Prais
Speak

'A powerful story of love, desire
significant impact technology has
MARY PORTAS

'There are three of us in this – you, me and your mobile.
How many couples have said this to each other? Paula Cocozza's
witty, wry new novel is sharp as a skewer about the devices and
desires in many modern marriages. I loved it'
AMANDA CRAIG, author of *The Golden Rule*

'A beguiling and unsettling modern love story, full of wit,
bafflement and razor-sharp swipes at modern desperation.
She loves her past; he loves his phone, the centre cannot hold'
LOUISA YOUNG, author of *A Year and a Day*

'A meticulously composed novel about getting and paying attention.
Paula Cocozza peels back the screens of modern life to explore
different types of distance – from those we love and from ourselves,
in a marriage and back to a lingering youthful relationship. Cool,
compelling, *Speak to Me* is both timeless and vividly contemporary'
RICHARD BEARD, author of *The Day That Went Missing*

'Cocozza is a perceptive and intuitive writer who is unafraid to
dwell in the life of the mind and, most crucially, the heart'
SHARLENE TEO, author of *Ponti*

'With a brilliant, thwarted woman at its heart, *Speak to Me* is a
novel of longing like no other. Cocozza's command of this narrative
voice is mesmerising – I read it at a sitting, entranced'
ELIZABETH McKENZIE, author of *The Dog of the North*

Paula Cocozza is a *Guardian* features writer who has written for a wide range of publications from the *TLS* to *Vogue*. She is the author of a previous novel, *How to Be Human*, which was published by Hutchinson in 2018 and shortlisted for the Desmond Elliot Prize.

SPEAK TO ME

PAULA COCOZZA

TINDER
PRESS

Copyright © 2023 Paula Cocozza

The right of Paula Cocozza to be identified as the Author of
the Work has been asserted by her in accordance with the
Copyright, Designs and Patents Act 1988.

First published in Great Britain in 2023 by Tinder Press
An imprint of HEADLINE PUBLISHING GROUP

First published in paperback in 2024 by Tinder Press
An imprint of HEADLINE PUBLISHING GROUP

1

Apart from any use permitted under UK copyright law, this publication may
only be reproduced, stored, or transmitted, in any form, or by any means,
with prior permission in writing of the publishers or, in the case of
reprographic production, in accordance with the terms of licences issued
by the Copyright Licensing Agency.

All characters in this publication are fictitious and any resemblance
to real persons, living or dead, is purely coincidental.

Cataloguing in Publication Data is available from the British Library

Mass Market Paperback ISBN 978 1 4722 9996 3

Typeset in Garamond by CC Book Production

Printed and bound in Great Britain by Clays Ltd, Elcograf S.p.A.

MIX
Paper | Supporting
responsible forestry
FSC® C104740

Headline's policy is to use papers that are natural, renewable and recyclable products
and made from wood grown in well-managed forests and other controlled sources.
The logging and manufacturing processes are expected to conform to
the environmental regulations of the country of origin.

HEADLINE PUBLISHING GROUP
An Hachette UK Company
Carmelite House
50 Victoria Embankment
London EC4Y 0DZ

www.headline.co.uk
www.hachette.co.uk

For all those who write
in the scraps of time
that the rest of life leaves

It has become clear to me that I will have to take serious action in regard to Wendy. Ten minutes ago, when Kurt's telephone vibrated with a wooden judder on the bedside table, his penis – there may be a more up-to-date word for it – winced. I received one small, sympathetic throb. Like a reply. I beg your pardon. I realise this may be too much intimacy when we've only just met, but the Forum is shut or empty, and there's nowhere else to go.

Kurt lay still. I lay still. The vibration stopped. A faint bluish patch landed on the ceiling above Kurt's back. His head cocked towards the bedside table, where a corresponding blue box lit Wendy's little screen. I pushed at his shoulders and unstuck my back from the sheet. This is exactly how last month's incident started too.

It makes my blood boil to think that earlier this evening I was the one who felt guilty. I carried my present from Kurt upstairs and hid it under the bed, where it would not bother me. Then I opened the window as wide as possible. I made sure it was fast. The street light flickered to life. Nothing else moved out there. No show at The Close this Sunday evening. I looked down on the front garden, on the crab apple and the borders of perfect, unpitted pebbles that edged the lawn, and my guilt grew. I wish I could shake this feeling, which is habitual with me. After all, tonight's debacle has proved my fears about Kurt and justified my preparations. Even when I drummed my heels on his calves to remind him where he was (inside me, Kurt), he did not recommence his movements but continued to stare at the bedside table. I do resent being incapacitated to no purpose. I clamped my hands on his ears and swivelled his head to face me. 'Look at me,' I breathed. Bear in mind that today is my fiftieth birthday. Happy birthday, dear me.

Kurt's head dropped. Sweat silvered the folds of his forehead, the tight pleats that puckered his eyelids. Outside air, I won't say fresh, slipped in through the window, a warm whiffle that blew on my toes, slinked up my shins and roused a few hairs I'd missed with the razor. That breeze was my call to action. Up bumped my hips, to jolt Kurt back – to me, in our master suite, at the front of the Beaufort, here in The Close. Third exit at the mini roundabout. You can drive straight over it. There's never anyone coming the other way.

Kurt picked up speed. I believe he wished to hasten to the end of our lovemaking. I squeezed my pelvis for all I was worth, to slow him, and to teach him the importance of being fully present during in-person communication. He cried out, his head swaying wildly from phone to me to phone. I found it especially injurious that Wendy and I lay parallel, both on our backs. *Might, be, ur, gent*, Kurt puffed.

I am urgent, Kurt, I thought. My urges are competing.

He glanced askance from beneath his russet lashes. His right eyelid pulsed, and I knew what he meant to do. He propped himself on one forearm, and as he adjusted his weight, I went for it. I got there first. I handed Wendy over his back, to my right hand. Like ninety per cent of humans, I'm right-handed. Alas, I had not allowed for the challenge of being horizontal. The phone bounced off the window frame, hit the sisal flooring – which I still think abrasive for a bedroom – and cracked apart.

Kurt spluttered, a guttural choke; I felt it spatter my forehead. He shrank, backed away from me on his hands and knees, then wordlessly dropped off the end of the bed. Crouching naked on his haunches, he began to reassemble that dreadful Wendy as intently as a troglodyte sharpening a flint. His oblivious buttocks and the sole of his supporting foot glowed amber in the street light. A head-to-heel rear view of sad, naked man. I wanted to visit the Forum right then, but that would have made me as dependent as Kurt. So I got up and came in here to the family bathroom to sit peacefully on the toilet. Just jotting down these thoughts is a comfort – as if someone else is out there listening. And, who knows, may one day answer.

Anyway, I don't need the Forum. I can recite their replies.

– Honey, you tried talking to him?

– Yawn in his goddam face.

3

– He's probably just bored. (!)

– When my gf did this I threw her phone out the window and said she gotta pick me or it.

– Break up if he does it a third time.

See, this is the problem, because tonight *is* the third time. When did it become not-OK to expect a person's full attention on a special occasion? I didn't get that memo. I know. Nobody sends memoranda nowadays. I didn't see the post, then. I wasn't in the right chat. And while we're at it, what sort of fiftieth birthday present is a briefcase? I know the leather is flawless, and Kurt has paid extra to have my own initials embossed on the lid. But when he slid the parcel across the kitchen table to me this morning, for a moment I thought . . . It was the right sort of shape. But it was too small, and too much, far too much, to hope for. And this is where I start to feel angry, because Kurt and I were fine. We were happy once upon a time, before the boys, before we moved here, before he became obsessed with his Wendys. Before I lost something I wanted to find. Oh, nothing major! Just an object I used to share my life with, which Kurt hates me to mention. I would like to discuss this with Kurt but as you can see, he is very busy and he 'can't not have a phone'. That's a quote. Well, we shall see about that. Kurt, I need to talk to you.

Too bad. His throaty snores drift evenly along the landing from our bedroom. Being holed up in the bathroom suits the occasion. I shall linger on the toilet and make the most of this chance to unpack my thoughts. It frightens me to think that we may have gone too far along our separate paths to get ourselves back to a good place together. I must recover my losses and find a way to free Kurt and me from Wendy.

How did we end up here?

Phase One

The day we quit our old house, something went missing. I knew this before I knew what it was. We emerged from a dark tunnel of trees on the main road and turned into our estate. The midsummer sun lit the pristine ivory surface of the new roads. I narrowed my eyes against the glare and took my foot off the pedal. The speed dial dropped below twenty. As we rolled around those bright, stupefying bends, I felt a seizing in my heart, a dread that dislodged itself and rattled and clinked like a stone in a can at each turn of the wheel. That stone kept knocking at me, it knocked and knocked till the knocks rang shrill. I braked. I hit the horn hard and let the boom blast those still streets while the boys screamed with delight and Kurt bit his lip. I'd left something terrible behind, and I feared I would never get it back.

The Close was – is – shaped like a keyhole. Our house is on the left, the last on the straight part before the road curves into the circle. I pulled over and let the engine run. We had driven for less than two hours, yet we had landed in a different country. Lamp posts rose weedless out of unstained pavements that glittered in the sunlight. No litter or petals blew in the gutter. The yellow parking line glistened freshly on the pale road. A stake had been set into our patch of lawn; I did not immediately discern the slender tree attached to it. I didn't see leaves, though this was late June. It was Kurt who finally reached across and moved the gearstick into neutral while the boys squawked and yanked at the door triggers. On the other side of The Close, an older couple watched us from their porch and waved. I don't know if you're aware, but people who live in cul-de-sacs are the happiest in Britain.

I knocked on Kurt's thigh with my knuckles and opened my hand for the house keys. His mobile telephone was in his lap, that special first smart one, which he had queued for overnight in the rain the previous autumn; and I remember that as he raised his hips to fish the keys from his jeans pocket, the phone, thick and dark and glassy, mirrored the sun, and slid in a bright flash between his legs onto the seat. It had not yet become the monster that I call Wendy. The keys dropped into my palm.

Our new house was a model known as the Beaufort. It was very new, especially to me. I had been too busy to visit the show home with Kurt and the boys, and the plans ill prepared me for the novelty inside. A twist of tissue paper sheathed each door knob and light switch. The whole place smelled as if it had been lifted from a box. The woodwork emitted a powdery, newly milled scent, the paintwork a tacky reek. Each footstep on the sisal carpet released a freshly sheared odour of blade and fibre dust. I picked the transparent plastic skin from the glazing in vast, floppy sheets. While the boys thundered up and down the stairs, hollering at their echoes, I pulled open cupboards, drawers, doors. They gave with a sticky peeling sound. I had the feeling the house had been sealed and was opening at my touch.

From the moment I stepped inside, I was looking for something. While we waited for the removal lorry to arrive, and Kurt and the boys played with the remote control, lifting and lowering the roller door to the garage, I went top to bottom with a tipping, keeling panic. I put this down to the stress of the move, a general anxiety about whether I'd remembered everything. Because there was nothing to find. How could there be? The house was box-fresh. The builders had left nothing. Not a hair in the paintwork. The closets held no ghosts. The stairs didn't creak. The banister didn't judder like our poor old one did, from all the times the boys had swung off it. Our new home was a blank slate, a house with no history and nothing to hide.

But I kept looking.

While the removal team parked, we allocated the bedrooms. There was one each for the boys, the master for us, and the spare (just the other side of this bathroom wall), which I planned to keep immaculate for nobody. From the window in there, I first saw our sad square of back garden. It's too dark to see it now, and anyway, I'd have to stand up. But I remember that our lonely young cherry tree looked faint against the bright tan of the rear fence, behind which lay a building site. I pictured the raw red bricks rising in subsequent phases to three storeys, to become the house behind our garden whose height Kurt had failed to take account of when he studied the estate layout on his devices. But on the day we moved, there was just a big hole. The builders had turned up their dance music; I could hear the vocals but I didn't recognise the language. A digger shuttled back and forth on the sludge that would yield the new house's garden.

I should say that the Beaufort is the most prestigious of the estate's five designs. It is shaped like a large box. All the rooms are square: boxes inside boxes. I had the sense that everything was in view yet nothing in plain sight. As the removal team filled the house with furniture and boxes, I felt the walls tighten around me. But I calmed myself and told myself that at least now there were places to search. Our neighbours Sally and Akhil were moving in the same day. Back and forth they trekked between a hire van and their Marlborough (some wit had named all the houses after dukedoms). As the afternoon wore on, the older couple opposite reappeared with a flask and camping chairs, which they set up on the verge outside their Clarence. Mick and Andrea were the first Phase One movers. For two months, they had been The Close's only inhabitants; it must have been amazing to see people.

We moved on a Friday. Over the weekend, Kurt and I straightened the boys' room. We had chosen the Beaufort so they wouldn't need to share, but they pleaded with us to move both beds into the room of the eldest (by a minute). I hung their clothes, folded T-shirts, picking my way across the floor, a soup of toys and games and sprawling limbs. I remember they were racing through the final Harry Potter; we had a waiting list of eighty-five at the library and I'd bought two paperbacks so both boys could read at once. Back then, the boys still read and played on the floor. They loved reading. They did. Nowadays they lie on their beds.

By the Monday, the sense that something was missing grew. Each time I shut my eyes, a small black hole appeared. I applied myself to seeing the best in our immaculate new home. It was a marvel to own so many cupboards, especially the vast three-door closet in the hall. A couple of evenings in that first week, after the diggers were done, Kurt and I slid aside the back doors and drank sparkling wine and filtered water on the 'terrace'. But the hole, that black hole in my mind, deepened at its core, and seeped and frilled, iridescent like an ink spot. It was there when I shut my eyes, it was there when I opened them. No matter how much I busied myself, or how often I tapped the magical soft-close kitchen cupboards, my loss sat there, a shadow at the edge of my vision. I could never clearly see it, and I could never not see it.

Well, life is full of missing. So I got on with it. In this state of knowing and not knowing, I organised the cupboards, hooked us up to the electrics, gas, broadband, learned the route to work and the boys' old school where they were to finish the year. And all the while, the dark in my head grew, soaking outward from the centre like a nib left to rest on soft paper. This is how gone things pass. When a thing vanishes from the material world, it slips into the mind of the person who owned it, where it lives as a cavity. But it's impossible to see what's lost because what's lost is gone. Am I making sense? I am trying. What I mean is, during that first week I believed I would unpack something to fill its shape and then I would feel OK. I would. But one night I sat bolt upright in bed. The duvet fell to my waist. My hair hung wet with sweat. And I saw it! The ink spot hid nothing. It did not mark the beginning of some mysterious neurosis. Nor was it a metaphor for an object I had yet to figure. That little blot was the true shape of my loss. I wanted to get up and start looking right then, but it was two in the morning and Kurt was asleep beside me.

———

The next day was Friday – my day off. I dressed early, and when Kurt woke, I told him I would finish the unpacking and organise the house. As soon as he and the boys left, I set upon the boxes. I felt sure I would find what I was looking for in each one I opened. The second box contained LPs, and after I'd unearthed my old stereo, I put on a disc I used to dance to in my student days. The scrape and clang of the diggers ricocheted around my head, so I turned the volume high – fresh perk of a detached house – and sang along as I bumped box after box down the stairs. Kurt had piled them in the spare room, but I wanted that room to feel ready for visitors. So down they all went. A cardboard maze grew around me. Stacks of boxes blocked the hall, the lounge, the drawing room – amusing idea, that there would be space to withdraw to in a house with two young boys. Twelve is still young.

I ripped the sticky sealing tape and tore off lids and out flew all sorts: a glass vase and a single roller skate, a machine to remove lint from sweaters, several cushions, which I hurled at the new L-shaped sofa Kurt had bought, bottles of head lice treatment, relics of primary school, candles and clocks, a plug-in globe, place mats and board games. The rubbish I bagged and drove out to the main road. Several times Andrea had hailed the refuse truck to let them know we were all here, but they maintained that our new postcode did not exist. There wasn't time to unpack *and* search. My hunt rampaged through the house. I filled empty boxes with things I'd removed from full boxes, and upturned others. I wasn't so much unpacking as vandalising. But I couldn't stop.

Precarious, random piles rose from the sisal, wobbly as those stone towers people build on pebble beaches. A brass carriage clock balanced on top of a cookery book, which see-sawed on the glass jar of the juicer we never used. There was a whole crate of teddy bears, a little sinister en masse. I scrawled 'LOFT' on the side of that one. And books. So many books. The Beaufort's only shelves were in the closet, where I managed to stow a metre or two of paperbacks. The rest I piled along one wall of the drawing room in what we call at work 'small stacks', which I hoped would stop Kurt from repeating his suggestion that I recycle them. I carried a crate of hand tools into the garage, quieter in there, thanks to the heavy steel door, and found the cellular blankets we swaddled the boys in as babies, folded next to the club hammer, claw hammer and sledgehammer, the tins of ancient nails and rusty tacks. Our old floor-length plum curtains didn't fit the Beaufort's windows, nor its style, which I would describe as confrontationally plain. Back in the lounge, I freed them from the boxes and they landed in stiff, craggy peaks like great brocaded mountains.

What was I looking for? Yes, I am coming to that. I still cannot understand how an object vanishes between one house and another. I can picture our boxes bobbing in the arms of our expert removal troops, out of our old door and into the truck, then out of the truck and up the pebble-lined path of the Beaufort. Could one have been left behind? In stories, things go missing deep in the forest, not in the middle of a brand-new housing estate.

Well, I will not throw a curtain over the events I am sharing. I admit: I was happy in our old house. Its cracks and crooked quirks held our family and our little misalignments intact. But Kurt, a project manager who built and oversaw websites for clients, was desperate to launch his start-up; which, if I have overheard correctly, is a back-to-front-end engineering and design laboratory. His big bugbear is that designers continue to prioritise the internet on desktop computers and treat mobile phones as an afterthought. Kurt reminded me that I believe a person should pursue their passions. And he supported me when I changed careers, when the boys were small. That is true. He did do that. I earned nothing for two years. On the other hand, a global recession was a terrible time to sell. Luckily for Kurt, our wonderful old house held its value much better than the new one, so we swapped our small Victorian terrace in south-west London for a heavily discounted four-bedroomed townhouse with integral garage on an unfinished estate in Berkshire. My commute to the large public library that I manage quadrupled – impossible now to cycle to work – but on the plus side, we had no mortgage, and Kurt's every waking hour could be spent on his widgets. I'm a little hazy on the specifics. I know he developed a sensual way to refresh without the need to drag down (a gesture he was convinced people would find cumulatively depressing), and he hoped that his simulated finger click would have a greater impact on our times than the like 'button'.

I tried to make the best of things. But that Friday when I wreaked havoc in the Beaufort, I felt ashamed, as if I'd misbehaved, though also still hopeful. So shortly before five, when I heard the car engine thrum on the drive, I crawled beneath one of those enormous brocade curtains and peeped out at the mess on the floor, and I waited for the three of them to come in and find me. Someone tripped entering the room – Kurt, because at the time the boys didn't swear indoors. There was a pause. I leapt out with a 'Ta-da!' and laughed because I felt so silly. The boys are not identical, but in that moment they wore the same expression of total bewilderment. Behind them, Kurt dropped his jaw and stared. 'I'm still organising this room!' I sang out. My youngest came to stand in the mess with me, and I marvelled at how easily he fitted in my arms, and I kissed the top of his head, which was right there under my chin. Our eldest turned and climbed the stairs, and I heard the click of the bedroom door.

That evening, the boys came to me in the kitchen, the youngest looking sheepish, to talk about bedtime. Our little routine had evolved over the years, but we had followed it since they were babies: a bath, into pyjamas, a story. Each evening I took it in turns whose bed I perched on to read; we went through so many books like that. But now the eldest did the talking, and what he said was: they had grown out of a story. My youngest silently lowered his head. All of the worlds seemed to run out of all of the books then.

Of course, I never did find what I was looking for. So for many weeks – who am I kidding? For many years – my loss felt indefinite, as if it might not be lost at all, and also that it just went on and on, a deepening, incompletable loss. I learned to live with it in a way that gave it substance. Something materialised out of all my searching. The box I never found was a box I daily pictured, whose contents I was free to imagine. It became a companion to me, a touchstone from my old life in the new house. Its absence, the way its absence bothered me, made the loss feel more present than it had felt in any of the years before. With a little effort, I could almost conjure it into the Beaufort.

I began to think about —

And this is a name I cannot say.

See, I think Kurt gave me that briefcase today – yesterday! Goodness, the corner of this screen says 00:25 – because he

18

wants to shut the lid on all this. But that is not how life works, Kurt. Things do not go away when you lock them in boxes or lose them or even replace them.

Oh no! Someone's coming. Footsteps pause outside the bathroom. A hand cranks the door handle. 'It's occupied!' I whisper. The feet pad lightly downstairs to the cloakroom, and I recognise my youngest (by a minute).

I must switch this little thing off and go to bed. A fine place this is to end a fiftieth birthday. In a minute, I will lay my body beside that of my sleeping husband, and try not to wonder too hard if I shall fall asleep myself. One last thing I want to say tonight: when I look back on our first few weeks in the Beaufort, it's those damn curtains I see, and me, lifting a hem or whisking them in the air, hoping against all reason that I would find what I wanted in the space beneath. I was so sure that one time I would fling up that brocade and see my old leather case.

It was about two feet long, half as wide, and deceptively deep. A diagonal gouge split the tan lid. That scar is someone else's story, for it was there when I bought it in a junk shop down one of those lanes near the covered market in Oxford, a strange little place that seemed out of its time. A bell tinkled when I opened the door, and I remember all prices were displayed in Roman numerals, including those for the few Roman coins the shop-keeper kept. This was in my second term as an undergraduate. Right there in the shop, the lid creaked when lifted, and for years the sound was magical to me. Only later did the creak trip the terror that I was giving myself away. Because after a certain point, I never managed to look inside that case without wishing it held more than it did.

I had been browsing for a while when the proprietor emerged from a room out back. Very traditional, in a canvas apron. He watched with a frown as I flipped the lid to and fro. Perhaps he worried I would weaken the hinge straps. 'Spanish hide. A rich, full grain.' He said it came from 'a very good house'. I didn't know about that. The front corners were scuffed, the dye peeling. I rubbed it with my thumb and my thumb turned russet. From beneath my fringe, I watched the shopkeeper shift from foot to foot. I knocked him down to twelve pounds fifty.

What else can I tell you? Goodness knows, a description would be helpful, and I have stared hard enough at it over the decades.

But let's see. My old trunk is edged with long pale stitches that nowadays will have come loose. Pardon me. 'Nowadays' is cancelled. Our assistant librarian, Mika, has put it in her round-up of old words we are to phase out of our communi-cations. I sent her on a (free) course to explore ways to attract visitors as we seek to justify our funding. Mika says we can say 'now' or 'these days' but I gather 'nowadays' is less now than 'now', and 'right now' is more now than either. I probably should not say 'pardon me' either. I will reread Mika's list, and ping or swipe-right her, or whatever the word is for dropping someone a line these days. My deputy, Susan, is riled by these changes, but I'm with Mika: young people find old words alienating, and the library would like to reach out to young people, and so would I.

Now, where was I?

My case. There is a handle. Perhaps most helpfully, the lid is embossed with the initials J.P.C. I liked storing my letters in a case that appeared not to belong to me. That was Antony – mine and not mine. You could say it of all lovers, but it was more true of him. Actually, I am not sure I did like the not-belonging, but what I mean is: the discomfort fitted me so well it was as if I had chosen it. In my mind's eye, the lid of that case is always ajar, Antony's letters spilling out.

So that's what I'd lost. Just an ancient case of ancient letters. And yes, I do know that when I say that, I am trying to squash down the lid, put all this back in the box. Back in the box.

Oh dear. There I go again. This is a habit I thought I'd mastered – describing my case to strangers, as if a description will help. It's this smart new one Kurt has given me that's making me behave a little desperately again. The first piece of fresh evidence I have obtained in nearly two years, and all day the thought of it has plagued me. Hence I've hurried home from work to examine it. Why would Kurt give me this? I swing it onto my desk. I have to push the catches so hard they dent my thumbs but at last the locks pop and the lid lifts silently.

Burgundy swirls swarm the interior, a rash of marbled claret picked out in gold, and I feel queasy looking into it, light-headed and scooped out. Propped against the back wall is a tiny card, like a florist's, on which Kurt has handwritten, with a rollerball he has borrowed from my desk, 'Sorry about your old one. This case is full of love & I will do all I can to help you keep it safe.' I wonder, when he wrote that 'sorry', if he wanted to apologise or sympathise. He has embossed S.B. on the lid. I think he intends it as the last nail in the old case. But I have no idea what to put in a trunk that is meant to be mine. And now that I have opened its sleek, glossy lid, I think of all that I've lost.

One thing I want to make clear is that this – document – is not about Antony, even if something of him occasionally escapes. It is not Antony I miss. It is something else, the something that slipped out of my life with my battered old case, and it is not him, though it would be easy to mistake it for him. No, Antony, if you're there, this is not about you.

Ah, there goes the roller door of the garage. Kurt is home. We need to talk about what happened last night. I will shut this down and continue tomorrow.

———

No, I will not continue tomorrow. I will continue right now. Because Kurt has come home with that damn slab of glass stuck to his hand, that small shiny coffin he is pouring us into, and he is standing in the doorway to this very room, not looking at me. He mouth-talks into his Wendy, which he holds perpendicular to his lips in the style he calls 'Crackerbread'. I know this because after he quit his job, he spent days in cafés and parks near our old house to observe how humans hold their telephones in the field. Yoo-hoo, Kurt. Over here, at the desk. Oh dear, I'm afraid he's neglected to give his nearest user visual feedback. He has forgotten his own mantra: a millisecond delay turns a user away. Type type, tap tap. Aren't you going to ask what I'm doing, Kurt? I'm keeping busy while I wait to speak to you.

Since Kurt is unavailable, I shall explain about our marriage. We have a modern version of a long-distance relationship. We share a house, but we live in different historical eras. Kurt, who

23

is two years older than me, has countless devices and re-spawns himself relentlessly. He is always the latest him, whilst I remain the same old me. I'm like a figure from a historical novel in my own drawing room – an anachronism searching for my moment. I do own this ancient laptop, though it is very slow; and for my birthday, I bought myself one of those clever phones that does more than make calls – but it is not at the vanguard like Kurt's and I keep forgetting where I put it. I left it in the bathroom last night when I finally went to bed. There are buttons in this room I do not know the consequences of pressing. I suspect there are many women in my situation, and that is why the Historical Fiction shelves at work always require so much tidying. Only Picture Books is messier, after a school visit.

Ah, at last! Kurt has finished his call. He lurks in the doorway, head drooping. You would think he sleeps standing up. But although his eyes appear shut, they are merely lowered; he is not sleeping but scrolling. He hates it if I talk to him when he is busy thumbing, tweeting, dragging, pinching, posting, sliding or swiping. It can be very hard to catch the moment when something is buffering. Since last night's incident, the only words he's addressed to me have been perfunctory texts about his arrival time and items we may need from 'outside'. I worry that the thing that is really buffering is me. I am stuck like one of those little beachball wheels that turns and turns and never comes full circle. I cannot go on like this. I push back my chair, and Kurt ducks into the hall.

Well, let him go.

I was saying that Kurt and I are physically closer than couples who live thousands of miles apart. We sit on the L-shaped sofa (occasionally the same prong). We share a bed. We fill the kettle to an even number of cups. We do not have to think, What time is it? where the other is. But something close to hand divides us. I shut my eyes when that thought comes: to hide the thought, or to see it better. Not looking can work both ways. And with my eyes shut, I try – I really try – to picture my husband.

No, I have failed again. I'm afraid all I can summon are Kurt's eyelids. They are the part of him that I know best. But when I fell in love with Kurt in the 1990s, people still looked into each other's eyes, and Kurt's were grey with pale yellow stars that skirted his pupils, and in those days, he looked at me, and I saw that he liked what he saw, and he would stop at my desk to talk and he was not coy or tactical. I was in the copywriting enclosure, next to the fax machine, and he was a website engineer, ahead of his time, and it was a novelty to me how plainly he asked me to dinner, and then another dinner. From our first date, he liked me openly. That felt so nice. I was starting again, with less than nothing, and Kurt's love felt – I suppose you could say restorative. But it was better than that. It just felt good in itself. I never worried back then that I would lose it. Looking at Kurt in the garden now, perched on the love seat with Wendy 'Crackerbread' to his ear, I have the sense that he has been remade many times since then. Wendy winks at me and gloats that it is back in one piece, and it has Kurt's ear.

I, on the other hand, have Kurt's eyelids. Those sad folds

of skin and muscle communicate with me when the rest of Kurt says nothing. The right one has a nervous pulse, like a hidden button. This is the eyelid I watch when I want an answer. Brown shadows, like bruises, press two sad moons below the sac of Kurt's lower lids. I expect he is deficient in something. It's possible his *levator palpebrae superioris* have broken. Given time, I am confident that humans, even slow ones like me, will devise new ways to communicate with our eyelids. Maybe my boys and their lovers will tattoo eyes on them, to foster a deeper connection. May their generation derive great pleasure from eyelids. May they fetishise them, may they eroticise them. May the poets of the future devote odes to them. Eyelids, the curtains of the soul!

Briefly Kurt glances at my window, and I snap him. I save the image to my new album, 'Kurt on His Phone in Beautiful Places'. I have added some old ones. Here he is with his little candy-bar phone at Tintagel castle. An almighty gust catches his curls, thick and lovely with sunshine, while the boys toddle adoringly at his feet. Unforeseeable that they would grow up to like grime. And say hello to Kurt as he checks his favourite websites in the ancient Greek theatre in Syracuse three years ago. He looked at his device so much that holiday, he got a tan line across his nose and cheek. And here is my personal favourite: Kurt thumbing his tiny buttons inside a giant Californian redwood during our trip of a lifetime, while the boys, eight, peep around his legs. I doubt he found reception inside a tree, but there is always something to look at.

At last, he has come indoors! The soles of his trainers squeak on the kitchen tiles. The fridge door unseals. Any second, he will look in here and we can speak.

It saddens me to admit that Kurt's voice has become grating to me. When I moved into his flat, a few months after that first dinner at Canopy, I would lie in bed each morning while he carried his radio from room to room. The engineers started their shifts earlier than us copywriters, and I loved to listen to that radio because I was really listening for Kurt. When it snapped silent, he would appear and kiss me goodbye. He didn't have a phone, of course: just the little blue pager. Now Kurt is the radio. On and on he drones, on these after-work work calls, blathering about the new security features he plans to install. I would switch him off if I could. I wouldn't want to turn him off if he spoke to me.

I open a search engine and type in the box: how long will Kurt be on the phone? There is a financial service centre called Kurt, and the search engine says that most callers wait no more than a minute. Unlike Kurt's wife, who has been waiting years. Why does Kurt prefer his phone to me? How can I attract Kurt's attention? Kurt, what have I lost that I used to have? Call me old-fashioned – no, don't, because I'm old enough to have seen fashion go out of fashion. Let me try again. I know this sounds old, or dead, but in the theatre of human relationships, I still believe the main parts belong to humans.

The house has fallen quiet. I did not notice that the ceiling no longer vibrates with the boys' low-pitched bass line and complex

27

beats. And I cannot hear Kurt's call, so I guess that too has ended. Or possibly – because there goes the chain – he has taken it to the family bathroom. Kurt has a special quiet place in the bowl he aims at, and he is happy for interlocutors to hear him flush. I know for a fact that he has taken a call from his mother while taking a shit. When I confronted him, he said she was going deaf.

I am beginning to think the Forum got it wrong about trying to talk. I do not know how to go about it with Kurt while he has Wendy. I can see only one way to manage it. I must get the two of them apart. Throwing Wendy at the window last night was my battle cry. Speak to me, Kurt, or I'm coming for Wendy.

One afternoon in particular marks an important development in this little history. Namely, the day I came clean with Kurt. It has entered my mind because I am in my office on the second floor – the best place for private reflection, being home to the reference bay (the remains of our reference library), Rare Books and the quiet room – turning over the events of last night. I'm afraid Kurt and I did not speak, and although I woke several times, I failed to find Wendy. And I am remembering that Wendy was not always a problem.

On the day to which I find myself returning, Kurt came in the front door, wiping the rain from his trainers. It must have been a Friday because it was lunchtime, and I was home. Kurt rents a desk space in town, a couple of miles away. It's possible he had bad news; I didn't have a chance to ask. A crash summoned me to the hall, where Kurt was kicking our boxes, which were really by then my boxes, out of his way. So I told him the bare truth. I told him how my Spanish leather case had gone missing when we moved, the one with the full-grain hide that had come from a very good house, and which I had kept for many years, since I was a student. He called it my 'Paddington' case when I first moved into his flat, and asked if I kept sandwiches in it (he hadn't read the books).

Kurt rallied to help. He rolled his shirt sleeves. He opened one box at a time, removed the items, passed them to me to unwrap. I'm going to say that this was five months after we moved, because we had decorated for Christmas, but it was not yet Christmas. My fingers flapped about in the base of each box to check it was truly empty. I behaved as if I thought there must be a false bottom, and I believe I did think that. Even when Kurt flattened them, I continued to think that something was kept back. Have you ever had that feeling? In the face of all evidence to the contrary, I was convinced that I would find what I was looking for. But, you see, I think hope was in each box. And hope, I have learned, needs very little space.

Kurt and I got on with the job. In the hall, I knelt, Kurt stooped, his new white grandad shirt falling forward with the weight in his chest pocket. After he quit his job to launch the start-up, he bought seven of these same shirts, to free the brain space he wasted getting dressed. Every few minutes, his pocket glowed. He was daft about that phone. We both were. He would pat his heart, not to check the phone was still there, just to pat it. He would take it out, light it up, watch it go dark, put it away. Ten minutes later, he would do it again. I imagine that's how early humans felt about fire. That thing was a wonder, and when it beeped or Rihanna sang, we both stopped whatever we were doing. Since my birthday on Sunday, Kurt has switched his latest Wendy, the slimmest in the world, to silent.

Excuse me one moment. There is a problem on the first floor.

Apologies. I have dispatched Gerald to assist our new self-service machine. Borrowers do keep running to the information desk. 'The machine says I need to come and speak to you.' This makes Susan testy, because the machine never says that. I have sent her to the sorting corner.

I was saying that some of the boxes Kurt and I unpacked had very mixed contents. Wrapped inside a tea towel was a transparent glass butterfly my mother-in-law had given me when Kurt and I got engaged. It had never looked much. But in our bright new kitchen, colour rippled its wings. I shouted to Kurt. I wanted him to take a photo to print for Maeve. As I say, it was a tremendous novelty, that phone, the most incredible tool. It didn't have buttons. One's own finger became a sort of stylus. I set the butterfly on the island; the two of us crowded around Kurt's hands as his fingertips brushed the screen. But although that phone was very smart in all sorts of ways, much smarter than mine, the camera let it down. Not a shimmer of rainbow showed in the photograph. We looked at the pictures, but it was just a sad old ghost butterfly. All we could see through the little glass wings was the side of the toaster.

We had only two boxes left when I reached into a deep one at the same time as Kurt, and found Kurt's fingers. The feel of them threw me. Warm and different. Not indifferent, is what I mean. I felt him go still, but still warm, waiting to see what would happen. I don't remember if we looked into each other's eyes, if that's something we did in those strange early months of Phase One, when we were all trying to raise the place to life. There was a rush of heat to my ears. I guess I went red. I kept hold of Kurt's hand, because it was something wonderful in my hand and it seemed to come from a much earlier time, when strangeness and love overlapped, when we knew each other barely, yet knew enough to see that love was beginning to grow.

Kurt must have been lost in the moment too, because when I finally let go of this amazing hand-held hand, marvellous relic from the pre-verbal age of communication, it swung down like a thing without will, and knocked heavily against the cardboard walls. It was the closest we came to talking about what we were doing, what either of us had done. Kurt never asked why the case mattered so much, or what I kept in it, and I, glad of his incuriosity, never asked why he helped.

He smiled at me and ran his fingers flamboyantly inside an empty box. He humoured my despair with his flourishes. I returned him a small, compliant smile, and he yelped. His hand flew out of the box.

He stuck his finger in his mouth and sucked it. A tiny bead of blood flowered in the small froth of saliva on his fingertip, as if he had been bitten. 'Are you OK?' I asked, reaching for the

32

box he had let fall. The interior was dark, and as I joggled it, I caught a faint rattle, as of a little thing moving lightly; something smaller than a pebble. Kurt beckoned impatiently, but I kept hold. Slowly I traced the cardboard base with my fingers, feeling into each corner, until my skin snagged on a fine, sharp splinter. I snared it under my fingernail, and wiped it gently into my palm.

A black sliver it is, like a dark tack, or a clipped claw, and although it is not as obviously shaped as some specimens, I could identify it in far more testing surroundings than the pale of my palm. I could have picked it out from a vast sweep of shingle. In that tiny shard I forgot the box house. I glimpsed the horizon. I smelled the sea. I saw another age. Of course, this little thing was millions of years old; but I mean to say I saw something from my own early ages. I held out my hand to show Kurt and I watched his face.

'A shark's tooth. I had a few of these,' I said. 'In my old case.'

Kurt puffed his cheeks and exhaled lengthily. The pulse surfaced on his right eyelid, twitched and vanished. The tooth – for I loved geology in my youth and I was sure that's what it was – slid into the valley between my middle and ring fingers. Kurt came to look. He bent over my palm, poked the tooth, shook his head. It was something the builders had left. It was a bit of old junk, one of the rusty tacks we'd inexplicably kept. And if I'm honest, I wasn't certain. I closed my fist and pocketed my hand. Later I zipped my tiny find into my purse. And I have to disagree with Kurt. True, it is an imperfect specimen – it's

33

missing a root lobe – but a tooth is what it is. I have a picture here, in one of these books I have 'borrowed' from Geology, and it is very persuasive to see the photograph and the tooth side by side.

Kurt left me in the hall. I heard the kitchen door to the garage clunk behind him, and all the levers lock into place. I guess he'd gone to tinker with his widgets. We had all but finished the unpacking. But I could not empty the last box. I pushed it, still sealed, into the corner of the drawing room and covered it with a brocade curtain. Kurt thought I was unable to accept that I fully lived in the Beaufort, but really I think I packed my hope into that last box, out of his sight, and for a while I lived with it, with the hope, as part of the furniture. I didn't know this then, but in our brand-new house, I had found a fossil.

In England, the Jurassic and Yorkshire coasts are known for fossil-hunting. However, Kent, where I grew up, has a quieter share of the spoils. When I was sixteen, my mother transferred me to a school in the next town. Although I had done well academically, I had few friends, and she believed me the victim of bullying. I was not bullied. I was merely ignored, and I understood that. We just didn't have what other kids had.

It took weeks to settle into the new school. You could hardly blame the students for failing to notice me. I was one of those teenagers cardiganed into obscurity. Speaking aloud was like a second language for me. I hated even to say my name. If only I could have said Suzanne or Susanna or Suze, with its sixties ring, all much more interesting than mine. But I would never have helped myself like that. Names, like all belongings, were to be given not taken. I know sixteen is very young, and all this happened a long time ago, but please bear with me. Stories of young love never get old.

One day after English, I was slow to put away my books.

It was an unseasonably sunny afternoon in autumn term. I'd chosen a seat by the window and the heat made me drowsy. I stirred myself and began to stuff my library books into my bag while my classmates trudged out of the room. A student from the next class perched on the front of my desk. Before I saw him, I saw his shadow fall across the bright pages of my pad. I clocked the patch on the waistband of his jeans (he wore Lee) and the cream cheesecloth shirt through which the tan of his skin seeped. I imagine few people know those patches are called jacrons. The understanding that his proximity should not be taken for an interest in me was part of my first sight of him. He had an air of accident. He held his back to me, held forth to his friends. I slipped my things into my bag more quietly, stole a glance at the back of his head – blond hair strictly combed back, the fine V of sun-bleached hairs on his nape like a salt line. He was unlike anyone I had seen. I knew he would take a lot of working out. To me he stood out as different, and insensible to his difference. Maybe this is just how self-acceptance looks.

All my books but one were in my bag when he jumped off the desk and spun to face me, as if he had only that second sensed another person behind him. His eyes glittered cool and inviting. I don't care if it sounds cheesy, I saw the sea in them. I did. The last of my classmates filed into the corridor. Seeing me still seated – I hadn't wished to scrape back my chair and draw attention to myself, an idea that at the time appalled me – he smiled, lifted my library book from my hands and flipped it over. "'A beautiful and intelligent young woman . . . affronting her destiny",' he read aloud from the back cover. 'How does that work in practice?' He spoke as if he knew me, though I was certain we'd not met. He had an incredible charisma that drew my attention away from everything, including the fact that he suffered from acne. Somehow he made you see him as he would be without it.

I shrugged. 'She'll demolish you with a cup of tea and a parasol. She'll keep you interested,' I said. 'Even when she doesn't care to.'

'Do you think I'll like it?'

I knew nothing about him or his tastes. I studied his eyes. 'You might. It's hard work, but worth it.'

He flicked the pages. The school library stamp sailed by in an inky blur on the fore edges. I saw him glance up when his teacher entered the room, but he continued to read while the teacher laid his briefcase on the desk and wiped the blackboard. (In those days, they made boards interactive with sticks of chalk.) I remember that the novel was *The Portrait of a Lady*, which my class was studying. She was another young woman who liked to lose herself in a book and was considered poor.

The room began to quiet. I said, 'There's more copies in the library.' I should know. I practically lived there. One last student entered and closed the door behind her. This amused – well, I didn't yet know Antony's name, because although he had asked about the novel, he had not introduced himself. I began to panic. 'I've got to go,' I said, and reached for the book. He kept hold. We held two corners each. I had no choice. I tugged it hard from his hands. Antony grinned. I'd got the book, but he looked victorious. I followed his gaze to the teacher, who was labelling a diagram of earth's inner core on the board. Knees bent, elbow patch vigorously bobbing, he wrote and underlined three times: HIGHLY MAGNETIC. Antony raised an eyebrow at me. I felt conspicuous, as if all my lights were switched on. Not a sensation I generally enjoyed. But Antony made me feel that it was OK to be seen. The teacher turned to face the class, clapping chalk dust from his hands. Antony took his seat, and I looped my bag over my shoulder and crossed the room to the door. The tiers of my peasant skirt swished lightly from my hips. People watched me go, and for once I didn't mind.

Finding that shark's tooth in the Beaufort made me jumpy. I held it in my palm that afternoon, and I saw the horizon, and I stepped outside while the pale wintry sun lowered over The Close, and I paced our garden path, picturing the day we moved five months earlier. The clouds had cleared, though it was bitterly cold, and some ancient instinct made me stoop to pick through the little beach of stones beside our path, glossy and rich from the rain. I grew up beside a shingle beach, hence I am drawn to pebbles.

Years ago it was explained to me – and I have read this again just now in Geology, cross-checked in Folklore – that a stone with a hole running through it has the power to cure a person of pain. Alas, there was nothing like that among the Beaufort's decorative pebbles. But there was more variety than you might expect in builder's shingle, and I felt heartened, because if I had found a shark's tooth, if I had, what else might I find?

After I exhausted our pebbles, I walked into Sally and Akhil's garden and poked at theirs. We had moved the same day. Might my case have wandered into their Marlborough? I rang the bell and turned away from the door. I don't know why it is that on another person's threshold I always prepare for disappointment. Someone was coming! I took another step back. 'Don't go! Don't go!' Akhil called. There was a scuffle. The chain jangled wildly as he tugged at the latch, and then he began to hammer on the other side of the door, as if he wanted me to open it. Poor Akhil. Phase One was very hard for our neighbours in Marlboroughs. Those doors were too large for their frames. On very hot mornings when we first arrived, I would see Akhil climb out of the lounge window in his suit.

'When I say *one*, push hard with your shoulder!' he shouted through the door. 'Three . . . two . . .'

I pushed, Akhil pulled, and Sally clapped as I fell into the hall. Akhil ushered me into their lounge. It was smaller than ours, with a two-person sofa and one compact armchair, so that when we sat, our knees touched the coffee table. I didn't see a mobile phone. My old one, in my pocket, weighed down the right side of my cardigan, and I had to keep straightening it, and my conscience. Sally was the chatty one, but they both looked at each other when they spoke, and both looked at me, and maybe because of that, when Akhil brought in three mugs of tea, I told them about my case. Alas, they had unpacked months ago and found nothing that didn't belong to them.

'We lost a few bits,' Akhil said.

Sally laughed. 'I wish we'd lost more. This house looks way better empty.'

I finished my tea, and Akhil opened the window for me to climb out, and I began to walk the rim of The Close. Few newcomers had arrived in autumn. I passed empty house after empty house, and the dark windows looked so sad. I passed a house whose windows were lit, and it looked sadder. I reminded myself: I must make the best of it. A family called Frittelli had taken the Marlborough just beyond Sally and Akhil's, and I could hear their children arguing. Then the road curved into another unsold pair, and I approached the crown of The Close, where the Glossops had strung festoon bulbs across their facade. Theirs is a Beaufort too, on a wider plot than ours, with a fan-shaped garden and a view from the living room like a seat in the stalls. The Glossops look over the keyhole itself, you see – that sad circle where all the lost souls come to perform their U-turns.

Goodness, it's gone five p.m.! I must have spent longer than I thought revising Mika's marketing proposals.

Suffice to say that Belle Glossop caught me gawping at their lights and came onto the drive to talk in a pair of very voluptuous house slippers. She had seen me from her bedroom window; she loved to look down The Close to the sunset. I had nothing to say to Belle Glossop and maybe that is why I told her I was looking for my case. I regretted it immediately. She did not ask, 'Where did you last see it?' or 'What does it look like?' She did not say she would keep her eyes open. No. She asked what was in it.

I excused myself and kept walking. Mick and Andrea from the opposite side of the straight bit had planted an engineered tree next to their scrawny crab apple, its limbs weighed down with unpecked bird-feeders. Alas in three phases, I have not heard a bird sing in The Close, nor seen any winged thing (save the glass butterfly). It can take many phases for wildlife to move in. Which is strange, because from up here on the second floor, I can hear the sparrows going berserk in the bushes on the library forecourt. I walked west out of The Close, wondering if Belle Glossop was watching me, straight over the cobbled mini roundabout where the welcome flags rippled and clinked like sails. After five minutes, the road ran out of surface. I leaned against the orange barriers, looking past the mouths of diggers frozen in the field mid-gape, and I watched the sun sink.

Every June when the boys were small, we rented a cottage in Anglesey, and after their bath, we wrapped them in blankets and carried them, one each, down the steps to the beach. We'd pick a rock to perch on – I'm thinking it would have been a piece of metamorphic bedrock – and drift into our own worlds while the sun set. I'd make up a story, then we'd carry them back up the steps. Often they would fall asleep and not stir even when we unstuck their shoe straps and slipped them into bed. The sport for me was to catch the moment the sun vanished. You can count the arcminutes with an outstretched hand, you know. But it is very hard to tell if what you are seeing is the last sliver of sun or the reflection of what has already passed. My suspicion is that the eye believes it can see the sun long after the sun has gone.

I left the barriers. To the north, they were building The Old Gables, but I didn't bother going to look, and it always felt so pitiful to walk to the show home and back. I turned towards

42

The Close. Dusk had settled, and as soon as I crossed the mini roundabout, I saw our box house aglow with all the lamps I'd bought to soften its edges. I stepped inside, but the familiar feeling that something was missing had got there first. I went out again after dinner. This time I veered left at the roundabout and walked to the junction with the main road, where we had first turned into this life, and watched the occasional car pass beneath the bare trees. It was always so hard to go 'out', as we say. Some sort of force field seemed to bound the estate. Beyond the bus stop and postbox on the main road, there was nowhere to walk. Besides, wherever you went, you had to come back.

I got home after ten. The lounge was silent. I supposed Kurt was busy with Wendy. I nudged the door and dispatched a 'goodnight' through the crack, eyeing the plum brocade in the corner, wondering what else I might find under there. I picked the little tack tooth out of my pocket and felt the world grow large again in my palm, as if my much younger self had handed my older self this lifeline, or opened what the boys call a portal. I would not be stuck here for ever. Writing this, I see that I let my hopes go far too quickly. Looking at these books, and at the array of images I have got up in various windows, I am certain that what I have in my palm is a shark's tooth. But at the time, I accepted Kurt's doubts, and my loss, far too readily. In my heart I felt that any loss was what I deserved.

Upstairs, the boys were fast asleep, so I kissed them. Each night since they'd terminated our bedtime story, the youngest had leaned over the banister to drop a 'night, Mum' down the stairs, and if I was quick enough, I would see a flop of fringe, a shadow on the white wall. But not tonight. When I got into bed, my mobile beeped. It was Kurt telling me he loved me. Ten minutes later, it beeped again. It was Kurt asking if I loved him.

Oh God, here comes my deputy, Susan. I will send her to tidy Historical Fiction.

What an ordeal.

She has gone – but only after complaining bitterly about a prize-winning novel that keeps turning up in Historical Fiction, where Susan insists it doesn't belong. She suspects a guerrilla campaign by a borrower. The book is set during the Thatcher years, whereas Susan adheres to the sixty-year rule for historical fiction. As an idea, given that we are striving to reach new audiences, this seems pretty . . . I want to say old. I mean, 'historical' fiction is not simply a matter of dates, but of emotional distance and also, these days, the pace of technological progress. I mean, how long until 2011 sounds ancient? This is what I asked Susan, who regards herself as an expert in the field, and who reminds me of one of those sinister female servants who haunt the genre, especially when she narrows her eyes and says that Melvil Dewey would turn in his grave.

Mind you, he might if he could see me here, so-called librarian frittering away hours on the World Wide Web. Let me clear these overlapping windows: the photographs of shark's teeth, a geological survey of Anglesey, and a treatise on the microstratigraphic evidence of the first human use of fire. I am going home. I must narrow my focus: on the Beaufort, and on Kurt. I press the shark's tooth to my lips, and smell the salt.

In the new year, a month or two after I found the tooth, we visited Maeve. Since Kurt's sister moved to Spain, I believe Kurt feels responsible for his mother. She lives five miles from us in what estate agents call 'a bungalow of character'. Mind you, they call this place 'an executive townhouse'. We had finished lunch, and I was showing Maeve the library books I'd brought for her, while Kurt and the boys braved the icy wind to kick a ball about the lawn. This was shortly before their thirteenth birthdays, and they did not yet own smartphones, and still played outside. I expect the boys are upstairs now, lying on their beds. I'm sure they are in, because when I got home from the library half an hour ago, their doors were shut, and I haven't seen them go out. I would have, because the little porthole window overlooks the drive. I have ventured into the garage, you see. It is Kurt's nerve centre – a blind spot for me – and, well, here I am. I must say, he has set it up very nicely. There is a padded stool, and a row of plugs and power banks. Very handy. This ancient laptop always needs charging.

Well, now, after lunch I started to tell Maeve about my case. She was the only person left to ask. I mentioned the love faxes Kurt sent me at work when we first dated. And by the way, Maeve had absolutely no difficulty hearing me. As I was speaking, I became excited. I remembered that several times when the boys were younger, and Kurt was organising the loft, he had driven over to Maeve's with a bootload of stuff, and the boys, to give me a break. So when Maeve went to the lounge for her doze, I made for the spare room. I lay on her shaggy carpet and looked under the bed.

The pungent reek of lavender, which Maeve dabs on all her things, rushed at me. I twisted my head and took another gulp of air before I turned back. A moment passed as my eyes adjusted to the dimness beneath the bed. I saw orthopaedic boots laid flat, those vacuum bags stuffed with who knows what, a baseball bat. She hadn't sealed the bags properly and they puffed against the bed. I was about to get up and look from the other side when I felt Kurt's hands on my hips. I screamed. They rested there briefly, possibly in shock too. And then gently but firmly he pulled me back from the bed. He kept one hand on my back while I lay on the floor, as if I might escape. Raising myself to my knees, I saw my own rough shape flattened in his mother's long-pile. My face was flushed from having my head bent low and I was gasping from that awful lavender.

'What are you doing?' I exclaimed. My eyes darted about the room. Kurt had caught me far too soon. One wardrobe door was open, and inside I saw the roller skate whose pair I had stuffed into our hall closet. I moved to stand, but he held me tighter.

'The missing skate!' I protested. I don't know why I fussed. All they ever do is roll off the shelf.

Just then Maeve appeared in the doorway. I believe she thought she had caught us mid-embrace, because she gave us a reproving look as we scrambled to our feet, and behind her the boys also looked disgusted, then contemptuous when Kurt tried to distract them with a roller skate in which they had long lost interest.

When we got home, Kurt phoned Maeve and told her I'd found my case. I stood in the kitchen while he and Wendy made the call. I was barely a glance over the neck of his beer. After he hung up, he held my gaze. We stood at opposite ends of the island and his eyes were as flat and dull as the underside of a pan. I waited for the rebuke. Instead, his jaw relaxed. My own shoulders dropped, and I saw something in his eyes that I had not seen in a while. I warmed to the familiarity, without fully placing it, and then I panicked. This was how Kurt looked when he was about to speak. I thought, My God, he is going to ask me.

'Just old letters. Some from my dad. My nan. I want it back,' I blurted. What could I say? Kurt hated to talk about the past, and I felt as if we had lived our marriage with the lid jammed down; him not asking, me not telling, and somehow our with-holdings had held us.

I wanted to say 'Antony. Antony was in the case.' Well, he

was. But I was still working out how to divide honesty between honest feelings and honest words. And there were other things too. All my old letters, my life. That makes me sound old. I was not old. I was forty-seven. I am barely fifty now, for goodness' sake. I searched for the words to tell Kurt that I'd lost something of myself I wanted to find. An instruction. A permission. An invitation. An apology. My guilt and shame were in that case. And shut up there, locked inside the smallest box, some sort of hope.

'My youth was in that case,' I said. It was one of the things.

Kurt smiled. (This was before he lost his patience.)

I do not know how Kurt feels about any of this now. Indeed, I have begun to wonder, perched here in the midst of his things, if I do not know Kurt. This generation of Kurt. His workbench is Wendy's walk-in wardrobe. Several sizes of little black power banks are plugged into Kurt's sockets. There is a leather sleeve – black leather, what a cliché – a grey silicone case, a snakeskin-print one that opens like a book, a box of Wendy's wipes, cable ties and a tiny stand like a little aluminium armchair. Further along, Kurt has arranged his bicycle oils in height order: dry oils and wet oils, five cans each offering something different. At the far end of the bench, near the kitchen door, there's the crate of hammers and tools. The box cutter was his weapon when he asserted himself over the unpacking, but I tested the blade against my thumb soon after I came in here and it was surprisingly blunt. The only piece of paper in the entire workspace is taped to the bricks:

a photograph of the four of us at a diner called Buck's, fudge sundaes as big as our heads, weird stuff on the walls. We went there on our way to the redwoods.

After our visit to Maeve's, my quest consumed me in ever more fantastical ways. I reported my case missing to the removal company. I called the estate agent, and asked him to call the people who had bought our old house. I asked my mother, though she had never visited the Beaufort, and really it was silly to ask her for help. I asked my friends, my sister Tam. I asked them all to check their houses, and then I asked again. Each kindly reply I treated with a great deal of scepticism. I even called the police. I wanted to ask Antony. It was his loss as much as mine.

I tracked down through the library network a self-help book called *Losers Weepers*, and ordered a copy. This little book lists strategies for locating mislaid objects, including a grid on which to chart 'appearances and disappearances'. The cover shows a woman victoriously holding aloft two matching gloves. I am clearly not the only person who loses things, because it has been borrowed eleven times. Unfortunately, it is now chronically overdue despite Gerald escalating the penalty notices. I do recall that the book said, and this felt ominous, 'People who continuously lose things risk making poor life choices.' It also warned: 'Watch out for low energy, forgetfulness, loss of appetite, insomnia and excessive sweating ... Persistent and long-term misplacement of objects, especially of the same object, can indicate depression or dementia (consult a healthcare professional).' I tried to think if I was losing other things: Kurt, the boys.

Kurt begged me to stop looking. When he caught me with my head in the closet because I'd failed to hear his key in the door, he grunted and strode to the kitchen, or up the stairs to game with the boys, who were never asleep when they should have been. Despite my protestations, he bought them smartphones for their thirteenth birthdays, arguing that early adopters thrive, and surely I didn't want them to be left behind. I still hate this idea, because who will be the adult in the room when all the adults and children are busy looking at their phones? Kurt never asked me the big questions. He did not say: What was in your case that mattered so much? Why can't you stop? Why can't you be happy, in this brand-new house, we four the corners of this light and airy square new life? He sent me texts urging me to move on.

As Phase One matured, the estate sped up its westward spread. The noise remained constant, but it came from further off. Around this time, I noticed a change in the way Kurt looked at me, on the occasions when he looked up from Wendy. It maddened me that he winced any time I lapsed and rearranged the enormous closet outside the kitchen. I did not say to him, but Kurt, you are one of the worst losers of things I know. In our old house you were always shouting had I seen your keys, mobile, wallet, cycling clip, earphones – oh, all right, earbuds! – Palm, stylus, membership card for the video shop. It rented DVDs but we both called it that, right until it folded. My husband ought to have understood the mental derangement that accompanies even small, recoverable losses. Truly I felt as if another, an inner, life had been sucked out of me.

Do you know what sitting here in Kurt's headquarters makes me wonder? How would Kurt feel if Wendy went missing? Would he hold himself together, as I have done these past three years? He would not. He has forgotten how to live without that insidious handmaid to nudge, manage and monitor him. I honestly struggle to think what the point is of a box cutter that feels blunt. I am fidgeting really when I poke and waggle it at the front of Wendy's black leather number and draw down the blade. The long pale wound takes me aback. It surprises me to see how deadly serious I am. But I believe that only the direct experience of loss will open the wonder of empathy to Kurt.

———

Kurt wakes at six thirty. All night he keeps Wendy under the pillow and sleeps with one hand upon it. How he maintains this hold when he turns over is beyond me. But if anyone touches his arm or tries to lift the pillow, he spins away, draws up his knees and tightens Wendy to his chest. In the morning, before he surfaces, he removes Wendy's night mode – he can do this one-handed without looking – then he notifies himself of the important things that have happened while he slept.

Sometimes Kurt speaks to Wendy and Wendy replies with

a woman's voice. In this melee, Kurt grabs his boxers from the top drawer and takes Wendy to the en suite, where he opens his bowels, shaves, showers and brushes his teeth while checking his feeds and ensuring his handles are in good working order. Kurt is a great planner. Each night he leaves his trainers beneath the bedroom chair, his jeans across the backrest. So when he re-enters the bedroom in a cloud of steam, he can hook a finger through the loops and step into each leg while palming Wendy. Next he threads an arm and phone down his shirt sleeve; he has gone back to the plaid ones he wore before we moved. Finally, he sits on the bed and – this is where I grow very excited – *lays down the phone*. For a minute or two, Wendy is prone and unhandled on the duvet, jiggling lightly while Kurt pulls on his socks.

I cannot approach Wendy from the front or Kurt will see me, as he did two days ago. It is impossible to sneak up from behind without disturbing the mattress, though I have experimented while Kurt bends disorientated over his feet. This morning I sat beside him and flicked open my dressing gown to cover Wendy, but Kurt abandoned his socks and swooped with both hands, adopting the position he calls 'the Cradle'. I am beginning to despair.

When dressed, he retrieves his bike from the garage; he cycles to the workspace in town, to the station if he is meeting potential investors. The roller door rouses itself with a quiet click-click, then slithers shut behind him. It is the last I hear of him till evening. We dine separately. The boys take their plates to the console, and Kurt returns late. However, the past few nights I have sat with him at the kitchen table. I've watched in silence while he eats with a phone and fork, an adaptation that allows him to charge his stomach with one hand while undertaking all the important life-sustaining tasks with the other. It has irked me to recall that my mother frequently scolded me for reading a book at the table. She did! She thought I was addicted. I wish I could have told her that books take us into ourselves in a way that makes us more alive and connected than ever. I suppose it's possible she wanted a conversation.

After dinner, Kurt takes the main prong of the L and 'works' while he watches TV, or comes out here to oil his bicycle or sit on this stool, with his laptop on the bench and Wendy perched beside him in the little aluminium throne. Sitting in this garage has opened my eyes to a simple truth: charging is Wendy's greatest vulnerability. In those moments, Wendy is powerless. Wendy is tethered. Of course, Kurt is there too. Because Wendy must always be to hand. He left the door to the en suite open last night, and I can tell you he pisses, pardon me, no don't pardon me, with his cock in one hand and Wendy in the other.

I wonder if I should step up my efforts to free Kurt from Wendy while he sleeps. One of the women in the Forum managed it this way on her seventeenth attempt. Coryphe says not to sweat it, my moment is coming, and I do agree with her. But what does she mean when she says I can trigger a moment if I create my own chaos? I have replied to ask, but she has not got back to me. One thing I know from experience, and I have shared this with the Forum: when I get hold of Wendy, I must explain my reasoning to Kurt, so we can talk. Otherwise he will immediately replace Wendy and fail to benefit from the adventure of separation. For the record, it is not because I think Kurt is having an affair that I want to take his phone. The phone is the third party here. I want to take it so he can't have it. When I take it, Kurt will have to speak to me, and he will have to help me lay hold of my fine-grained leather case.

There goes the click-click of the garage door. I must get out of here.

———

We were nearing our first anniversary in the Beaufort when Kurt appeared with our box cutter and said it was time to finish the unpacking. Anyone could see that my brocade 'table' was at odds with the plainness of the decor, as if we had rented out a corner of the drawing room to a magician. I suppose that was the point. Maybe I'd pull out my old case like a rabbit from a hat. He whipped off the curtain and carried it to the garage.

The last box was brown and taped like all the others, with the name of the removal company printed on its sides. It did not look singular or promising: an unlikely vessel in which to have stowed so much hope. Kurt returned. He squatted on the drawing room rug and spun the box between his knees. He gave a small shrug. He wanted me to know that my Spanish leather case would not be inside, and that in a few minutes, when we could see the bottom of the box, or when we had removed enough objects to leave too small a space, I would need to accept that sometimes in life what is lost cannot be recovered. Kurt reached for the blade to split the tape, and the ripping sound brought me to my knees.

The package he pulled out was flat, wrapped in newspaper, and I felt myself warm to this object whose dimensions allowed me to imagine for a few moments more that good things lay beneath. Kurt began to peel the newspaper, and I knew what it hid as soon as I saw the gilt frame. It startled me, and How strange, I thought, as I took it from Kurt's hands, that we had nearly got to the end of Phase One on the estate without either of us having noticed it missing, this photograph of us on our wedding day. The wind had caught my veil and I'd reached to grab it with one hand. I wore a bias-cut dress to accommodate my bump. Wendy, of course, had not yet been thought of, but I recall Kurt entrusted his candy-bar phone to Tam, with instructions not to play Snake. I wonder how many people will say their vows today with their phones in their pockets?

If I turn in my chair this minute, here at my desk, I can see Kurt. Did I mention? He has entered the lounge. The doors between these two receptions fold back, you see, to make the space flexible. One of the architect's illustrations showed a party in here. Tonight Kurt sits on the main prong of the sofa, his phone on his chest like a baby after a feed (I think he calls this one 'the Nurse'), his laptop on his lap and the remote beside him. It's a lot of nursing for one man. It is unspeakably sad to see him so consumed. But what can I do? My feet rest on the burgundy trunk, the perfect height, and my ancient laptop is primed with a whopping charge – God knows what Kurt feeds those power banks – and it is best that I carry on here. This is not so unlike speaking.

Kurt's right hand was invisible in our wedding photograph, but I knew it pressed the small of my back. And although the wind blew from right to left, and all the loose things flew that way, our bodies tipped towards each other, mine back against the wind. I unstuck the flap and stood the picture beside us on the rug. These days, it lives on a shelf in the bedroom, awaiting its next move.

Kurt removed object after object from the box, among them some long-lost books I'm ashamed to say I stole from the school library, still in their plastic sleeves, and a couple of the string pictures of boats my father enjoyed making, and remembered how to make, long after he had forgotten everything else. And then Kurt had his hands on the last thing from the last box and I braced myself for disappointment – it was an oven glove, wrapped in newspaper, and I have no idea which of us packed it so idiotically – but honestly it wasn't like that.

As he overturned the box to show me that there were no fossils, no stone relics, I experienced an expansive sensation in my chest, some new capacity opening up, and I gave the longest outward breath I've ever breathed while my hopes flew out of that box like a soul departing a body. Hope built a new box around me and I filled it. I felt, in an odd way, rehoused, right there on the rug, with those odds and ends dispersed around my knees. Any pain I experienced at the realisation that the case was not in the box was wrapped up in this sort of new home within our home. I watched Kurt and his look of commiseration with a beatific smile, because his pity, or was it remorse, stopped short of me. I saw it, but I would not admit it.

My loss was locked safely within me. I thought then that I could contain it. I would just hide it in myself and carry on. I would be the thing I hadn't unpacked, and I could live like that. Every family has a few forgotten boxes, and I could pass easily enough as a forgotten thing. I felt euphoric.

'Let's have a housewarming!' I cried.

The idea of celebrating a year after we moved made Kurt laugh. This was back when Kurt did laugh. He threw the flattened cardboard to the floor and with his foot nudged Dad's string pictures to clear a space. He grabbed my hand and pulled me to my feet. He reached towards his pocket for Wendy, which he used as a stereo as well as a telephone – but I stopped him. We had all the music we needed, the music in our heads. Kurt pulled me into his body and our bodies began to sway and we danced as we had danced at our wedding, with Kurt half-humming, the words a warm reverb in my ear, his toes toeing my toes. And we turned like that, my head on his shoulder, my nose in his neck, round and round and round we went, at home in each other.

It was a summer evening in July, but we hadn't lowered the blinds though it was darkening outside, and neighbours looking out of their windows on the other side of The Close and down into the keyhole must have seen us there, turning slowly in our illuminated box as if we had been fully wound and were now playing out our long tune. Every now and then I would feel Kurt's lungs rise and push against me and he would raise the chorus, and even though he knew too few words to sing, he mouthed music. His breath parted my hair. My scalp thrilled. You see, it was our first dance come out of the last box.

———————

It is very distracting, but all I can hear is Kurt drumming his phone. This current Wendy is extremely slim and stylish, silver and black, and despite its stunning lack of girth I gather jam-packed with pixels. Nothing like that first model he had in Phase One. His fingers patter its swanky posterior. I used to think this meant that he was checking Wendy for life, but it is his own pulse he has lost inside that silicone sleeve. He hands it over when he lays his finger on the home button.

I despise that phone, and it is making me despise Kurt.

I push back my chair, pass between the interconnecting doors and seize the remote. I pause the TV. Kurt must sense this is an act of communication, because he adjusts the lid of his laptop and plucks his phone from his chest. Ugh! Phone, phone . . . The word rings out from other words. Even on paper that thing is incapable of unobtrusiveness. Kurt raises an eye-brow at the still picture on the telly – he has learned to do this without lifting an eyelid. 'Hi, what's on social media tonight?'

I say. 'Want to watch it together?' He shakes his head dolefully and releases a long sigh that I fear may be the limit of his audio package. His phone is programmed to reward attention, whereas I am saying nothing new and my words are too wordy. I drop onto the sofa beside him and I tip my head towards his head until my eye nestles in the dark arc of his ear. It is my plea for attention. Talk to me, Kurt, and I will like you. Kurt says nothing, but he does not shake me off. Neither does he wriggle further along the L, though I detect tension in his right flank.

Good grief, he has stopped scrolling!

He throws back his head and stares at the ceiling; nothing to see there, not even a cornice.

He is going to put the phone down. I'm sure he is. Come on, Kurt. You can do it. He balances Wendy on his right thigh: dark, glossy, patient in an open-fronted silicone case. Kurt's head feels for mine, tips into my space. He may still love me, out the corner of his eye. His bicep clenches against my chest. His foot taps, and on his thigh Wendy begins to wobble. Kurt makes a pre-verbal sound, like 'da da da da da da da da'. I think he is trying to regulate. He grips Wendy, flips Wendy. It somersaults on his thigh. Glass, silicone, glass, silicone . . . Put Wendy face down, Kurt, and let go! My heart drums his bicep and Wendy bounces unmanned on his jeans while I wait to see how this game of phone roulette will end.

My victory looks precarious, and a small part of me would like to reach across and remove Wendy from Kurt's thigh and fling it onto the far prong of the L, then squeeze Kurt with both arms and hold him and maybe kiss him or straddle his legs and kiss him again less tentatively or something to celebrate and keep his hands busy. I'm thinking this is an unlikely course for the two of us when he lifts the remote control and unpauses the TV. That's OK, I think. TV we can do together. A moment later, his right hand retrieves Wendy from his thigh and passes it to his left hand, which snakes along the sofa cushions. Kurt is not totally insensitive. He honours our intimacy by holding the phone at arm's length, that its light may not disturb me.

He fidgets, busy elsewhere, but there's still the warmth of him, the end of a curl that tickles my brow. And I think, It should be possible, like this, to know a little better the insides of each other's heads. There should be some smart way to understand what's in there, to shut our eyes and human Bluetooth. This doesn't happen, of course. We don't have the headset for that yet. But we are so close, maybe something has been transmitted.

Oh Kurt, is it too late to switch us off and back on again?

Antony and I used to speak on the phone.

In the house where I grew up, the phone lived in the hall. When it rang, there would be an almighty thundering of feet as we girls raced to it from wherever we were. Except my little sister Jilly, who was always watching TV and never budged. Tam or I would pick up, then recite our number followed by the words 'Hello, who is it?' However, as we grew, we liked less and less to take our calls in the hall. We shut the lounge door so the noise of Jilly's telly didn't get in the way. Then we shut the porch door so the noise of the road didn't get in the way. Then we shut the kitchen door so the noise of the railway didn't get in the way. We shut as many doors as possible so everyone else in the house wouldn't get in the way, but my father hovered in the hall whenever the phone rang. He assumed – mostly correctly – that the call would be for him. If it was not for him, he would lean against the wall with his arms folded until he'd heard enough. There were never enough doors to shut.

We had one phone, and we called it the phone, and we

used it to take calls because taking them was cheaper than making them. In sixth form, after Dad left but before Mum moved us into the flat, I became more independent. When I wanted to talk, I slipped to the end of our road. The corner was home to a letter box and a phone box, all the boxes a human wishing to interact with other humans could need. It maddens us all here in The Close that the postbox has been deferred again, to Phase Four. We have to go 'out', as we say, to post anything.

Our childhood road was not a long road, but it ended far enough from the house that I could use the phone box without being seen by my family. I liked the privacy, but I still felt embarrassed each time I spoke into that receiver. The musty smell of other people's breath, the puddle in the uneven floor drying out, the crack on the pane of glass, the receiver sometimes warm from the person before, the person before sometimes still in the box so you had to wait outside trying not to listen . . . Other people at sixth form had two home phones, including Antony, whose family had a cordless handset that he was allowed to take to his bedroom. I always felt unworthy of Antony, and that damn phone was part of the feeling.

I dreaded his mother picking up. I worried each time she answered and heard my echoey voice, laced with the grime of passing traffic and trains, asking for her son, while trying not to sound panicked by the fact that however long it took her to fetch him would be time deducted from our conversation. It cost at least ten pence just to find out if he was home. They owned the large mint-green house on the seafront; all that space for Antony and his parents. Even now, thinking of Antony, I can smell the captive cigarette odours, the pleasant staleness of the slow-circling dial, especially when I got to the eight and the zero. The microphone part was shaped like a cup, and because I was small for my age, my nose as well as my mouth fitted inside. I inhaled Antony through the receiver. Later, when push-button phones replaced rotary dials, Antony's number, the pattern of it, became embedded in my memory. Even today I can summon the dial pad on my phone and my fingers fall into formation. I did ring the number at the end of Phase One, when I was arranging our housewarming, but the person who answered had never heard of Antony.

Did Antony know I called him from a phone box? I worried he could hear the coins dropping in and kept me talking just to see how much I was prepared to pay. Sometimes I was in the box so long, my mother came to the end of the road in her flip-flops (an early form of shower shoes, and they definitely were not a mark of technological genius as the boys insist they are), and rapped on the glass to tell me dinner was ready. That was not a good feeling. I try hard not to cramp the boys; I worry I may have gone too far the other way.

After pushing in all that money, I felt awfully empty-handed if I hung up without knowing when I would see Antony. My Saturday job cleaning offices paid £6.60. I'd watch the credit count down to the dreaded pips. There was always the question of whether to insert more. By ten, I'd start to panic. I'd say,

64

'What are you doing tomorrow after school?' and he'd launch into some story about whatever interesting thing – there always was an interesting thing – he planned. I had to pay extra to hear what it was. Then I'd mention some film I hoped to see – had hoped to see with him – and then I'd have to go and see the film alone, just to have something to talk about next time. And to prove that I did not depend on Antony to be interesting. For I must not depend on him, nor anyone.

I was an idiot then. I almost never asked if he wanted to go out. All those coins I pushed into the slot – I was really feeding my timidity. I tried not to think about how much I was spending on my friendship with Antony which, in any case, I had no power to end and which, at any cost, I wanted to go on and on.

Now I get more free calls than I have words to say, but who is there to ring? Phone calls are for cold callers and distant loved ones, like Tam (in west Wales with her current partner) and my mum, who finally has the cottage in Cornwall she always wanted; very occasionally Jilly, when the time difference works and I think of it. And I do understand – I have overheard the boys say – that it is not OK and kind of pressurising to expect another person to pick up.

Anyway, I don't need a phone now. You are my one, long, free call.

———

It had just started to spit one evening when I went to try Antony, and the glass in the phone box was speckled with moisture. I enjoyed being shut in there in the rain. It felt cosy, as if we'd zipped ourselves inside a tent. I watched my money count down and I said goodbye. He was going to the theatre the next night and I had pledged yet another trip to the cinema. I finished the call and trudged home, drizzle clinging to my hair.

Inside the house was chaos. My mother was yelling my name. My sister Tam was running from room to room looking for me, Jilly was watching TV, and in the hall the phone was ringing.

'For you,' Tam told me. She rolled her eyes and made a moony face. 'Third time he's called in two minutes.'

I took the receiver.

'Why did she tell me you were out?' he asked. He sounded hurt.

'I was. I've just got in.'

'Don't lie. You cut me off. I called right back, and your sister said you were out. She sounds just like you. It was you, wasn't it?'

'I was walking home from the phone box,' I told him.

I became aware of a silence on the line, in which I felt Antony grow stronger.

See, I never did own the channels of communication. Even today, when I have all the things a forward-thinking person is meant to have – social media, messaging applications – Antony owns those channels simply by not having them. I couldn't reach him even if I tried. When we moved here, and I was searching for my case, I did have a little poke about for mentions, a root around on Myspace. But nothing. He isn't on Twitter or Instagram or any of those. The only Facebook page that might be his has no public posts and a profile picture of a monkey. He comes up always in the same few search pages, including a cursory listing on the website of a theatrical agent, likely out of date. I must say, I find it incredibly painful to think that Antony may have died and not thought to tell me.

My mother clattered the plates on the table. A hush spread in the kitchen. I lowered my voice. 'Everyone's listening.'

My mother poked her head into the hall and barked that dinner was going cold.

'What was that?' I said to Antony.

'Do you fancy the theatre tomorrow? I've got two tickets for *The Birthday Party*. I wanted to ask but you said you were going to the cinema. I know you love going on your own, but it's a really good production and—'

I covered my free ear with my hand and waited for the express train to pass. 'Yes,' I whispered.

And that is how we started.

The next evening, I walked the coastal path to Antony's mint-green house in the next town. His town had a pier, and mine did not. I don't know why that seemed significant. Antony's father drove us to the prestigious touring theatre down the coast, and after the performance we made our way home on the train, just the two of us, then took the last mile along the beach very slowly, past the fishing boats, long since gone, with the pebbles crunching beneath our feet, our heads, our backs. When I finally got home and undressed in the bathroom, a shower of tiny stones clattered out of my underwear onto the lino.

There are places on the mobile internet where a person can search for a death certificate, but I cannot type more than a few letters of Antony's name into that box without fearing that the box is charmed, it is really a grave, and the act of entering the letters might make him dead.

The night that Kurt and I danced, the dance stopped.

A vibration in Kurt's breast pocket thrummed on my shoulder and jagged the needle across the song in my head. Kurt had different sensibilities back then, because he excused himself before taking his call – from the director of a prestigious conference that he had been invited to address. He unhooked himself from me, but intimacy leaves a warm aftermath and it was there in that room, and when he left, I waited while it cooled. Dancing, we had been lost in the moment. Now that we were lost in it no longer, we were more misplaced than before. Even today, at this late stage, I find it hard to judge the distance between us. We are so synchronised in our separateness.

I knelt on the drawing room floor, tidying newspaper and scouring the rug for shark's teeth. Kurt re-entered the room and crouched beside me, and laid Wendy beside him. In those days, he felt OK about doing that. We grouped the items we had unpacked according to the rooms they belonged to. Kurt headed to the kitchen, while I made an apron of my skirt and scooped into it the wedding photo, et cetera, and went upstairs. I could hear Kurt at the closet; one of the skates kept rolling out and he kept wedging it back. He was humming our wedding song. He sounded very happy. He did. I think it was that moment I wanted to keep. I shook my skirt over our bed. Out came the photo, a box of old jewellery, a glove, the three paperbacks I'd taken from sixth form – one of them was that ancient copy of *The Portrait of a Lady*, and by the way, it took her a very long time to affront her destiny, in fact I'm not certain that she did – and Kurt's phone.

It is unfortunate that I am at work today, because Kurt should really be here for this: these words are the closest thing to us talking. But bear with me. He will pop up soon. He just needs to load on my aged laptop. I could use a moment to recover from the commotion, because one borrower, a little older than me, has just broken into song in our reading room. Susan had warned me about this woman, whom she suspects is behind the dissent in Historical Fiction. As soon as this borrower – and I have told Susan we are not to call them that any more – saw me head towards the information desk after lunch, she stood and belted out the chorus of 'I'm Every Woman'. There was a lot of shushing, but not from me. I stayed on my feet. She has an incredibly powerful voice.

Ah, hello. There he is! Welcome to Kurt. It's the video of that talk I mentioned, the one he gave to the prestigious conference about eighteen months after we bought the Beaufort. Let's see. January 2010, it says, 'Refreshing Your Perspective' – and I am not the only one who likes it, because it has had more than eleven thousand views. Obviously this video is not the same as having Kurt here in person, but it is better than nothing. Think of my screen as a stage, and Kurt's little pop-up window as a box at the theatre. He can watch the next scene unfold.

Now, where was I?

Oh yes, that's right. Kurt re-entered the drawing room. He stopped humming. He stared at the rug. His hand went to his head. His feet went to the closet. The doors shut, opened, shut more slowly, opened. He clicked his onyx ring on the shelves. His footsteps fell uncertainly back to where I was tidying. Very little remained on the rug, but he lifted the objects to look beneath them, then almost immediately lifted the same objects. Then he lifted the rug. Every few seconds, he squeezed his empty chest pocket. He pushed his fingers into his jeans pockets, and to show sympathy, I did the same with my skirt. He went into the garage and checked, I presume, Wendy's walk-in wardrobe. I watched, fascinated. This is how Kurt behaves when he loses something he really loves.

He tried, of course, to phone his phone. This was the most stressful part for me. I followed him around the house, willing Wendy's battery to die. He had only a cursory peep in our bedroom, everything neat and tidy, and he scarcely glanced at the door of the en suite.

We ordered in curry. I had to ring for it, of course. (This was in the days before delivery apps.) Kurt loved my housewarming idea, which I believe he took as a sign that I had finally accepted the Beaufort. He suggested I choose a piece of furniture to put in the drawing room where the box had been – and that's how, a few weeks later, my desk arrived. It was amazing the way he looked at me facially that night, his cheek and jaw muscles helping to shape the sound and air stream into recognisable speech. I'm certain this conversation happened because Wendy wasn't there. In fact, it was during this conversation that I decided on the name Wendy. Privately, I mean. I may have been inspired by the character in *Peter Pan*; she had attachment issues.

Kurt and I agreed that I would organise the party. I had more time. I have Fridays off work, and as the boys grew, I stepped back from them. It hurt to do it, but it was what they wanted: if we left the estate, they bowed their hoods, walking so slowly I had to hang back or overtake, and overtaking meant losing even the sight of them. One Saturday I took them to the shopping centre, and as we left the shoe shop, I spotted a penny – a shiny one, the sort they used to pick up for luck. The boys looked up from their phones then back without breaking stride. They didn't shake their heads or say, 'Not interested, Mum.' They were thirteen, and they had no need of luck, or pennies, or me. I left the coin on the floor, and I haul up the memory here as from the bottom of a well.

The Kurt in the pop-up box, of course, understands none

of this. True to form, he is inches from everything and utterly oblivious. Late in Phase One, and even in Phase Two, I liked to watch this talk of Kurt's because it made me feel Kurt was talking to me. But today, I confess, it is the satisfaction of penning him in his own little box that I enjoy. I have shrunk his window. I keep him on mute. I know what he will say. And I know that when he licks his lips and reaches for his glass of water from the table beside the lectern he is approaching my favourite segment, at 5:34, about how the act of refreshing is the frontier between our remembering and experiencing selves. I'm not sure I agree with this, incidentally. I just like the way Kurt looks directly at the camera when he says it.

But I am letting the internet distract me.

I wish I could stop it doing that, because I was trying to bring to life something important.

After I took Wendy, I had to decide whether to come clean or leave the phone for Kurt to find. We had scarcely finished our curries when he became restless. Sweat moistened his hairline. He agitated his onyx ring. He crossed his arms and plucked and scratched at them. When I tried to draw him back to the party, he jumped off the sofa and shouted upstairs to offer the boys cash to unplug themselves and help look, which they did for a few minutes. I heard Kurt ransack the closet, and then there was a sort of sliding sound and a thud. I peeped into the hall and saw him on the floor, slumped against the closet with his head between his knees. He did not wish to leave that closet; he clung to it as if it held the answer.

73

Poor Kurt. I did feel bad for him. I helped him to his feet, and though it was scarcely after ten, he crawled upstairs. I listened for him while I cleared our plates and takeaway cartons, but I did not hear the bathroom tap or chain – a relief. When I crept into our bedroom, Kurt lay fast asleep on the duvet. I felt watchful, and very conscious of my good health, as if I were observing a person in a hospital bed. I felt that I was looking at him after an accident, and I felt uncomfortable that I had caused the hurt, and also that it was necessary. I untied his laces and placed his trainers beneath his chair. I dropped his socks in the basket in the en suite and I checked on Wendy. Its battery was dead, so I stuffed it back inside the same rolled towel, then I lay beside Kurt while I pondered how to return Wendy. The next morning, Kurt awoke to the noise of the rubbish truck in The Close, and leapt out of bed with a cry.

And this is where things went wrong, because at lunchtime, he texted to say he'd bought a new phone. He'd lasted less than fifteen hours alone – most of them asleep. And the new phone, which was all white, was very fast and much pushier than the previous Wendy, always telling him he had messages, look at this, look at that. So you see, I must be very careful how I part them. I must make Kurt understand. He will get Wendy back in one piece – after we have spoken.

While Kurt stayed late at his workspace with the new Wendy, I went into the back garden and dug a hole beneath the ornamental cherry. I realise this may sound fantastical, but I hated the idea that someone else would crack Kurt's refresh mission, his secret suite of touch gestures. Things surface in the rain, so I shovelled down more than a foot. What else could I do? Kurt had lost interest; Wendy was dead. I back-filled the hole and heeled the soil. Maybe one day the new owners, or the owners after that, planting crocuses at the base of a broad cherry, will find the phone and be tickled by its antiquity. Till then, may Wendy rest in peace.

They are all Wendy, of course. I refuse to individualise them. Kurt's current squeeze may look vulnerable, with its glass front and glass behind, yet it brags of its unbreakability, its custom casing that's stronger than sapphire, ten times tougher than plastic. I'm quoting Kurt here, bigging up Wendy with someone on the other end of Wendy, and sometimes I think Kurt repeats all this because he is daring me – daring me to act, to try to save the things that are breakable.

We held the housewarming party in October, fifteen months after we moved. When the bell rang with our first guest, I did think, *Antony*. Of course it was not Antony (it was my cousin Richard), and I doubt Antony even saw the invitation. I sent it by email to that theatrical agent I found online, but she never replied, nor did I hear from the alert Mika set for me, and really there was nothing to say that Antony was still with that agent. Indeed, there is nothing to say that Antony is still with us at all.

For the first few rings of the bell, his damn name pinged in my head – a sort of *Antony!* alert – and I sped to the door. There is no point looking out there now. There is nothing going on. But on the night of our party, the street throbbed with the sound of traffic, car radios, slamming doors and honking horns, the thrust and slack of engines as people backed and forwarded into tight spaces. It was wonderful. Our little dead end was criss-crossed with the beams of headlamps as guests helped themselves to the driveways of unsold houses and the turning circle became a car park in which everyone was boxed in. I left the door to Kurt and collared Richard in the kitchen.

Poor Richard didn't know a soul. In my excitement at remembering he was a detective inspector, I had forgotten to invite his family. He regaled me over the top of his beer with jokey insinuations about why he had been chosen, while I apologised for having neglected his mother, my aunt Barbara, who had spent the month since Richard received his invitation wondering what she had done to offend me. What am I saying? No one says 'invitation' any more. You must have noticed. I'll ask Mika to add it to next week's list.

Our lounge and drawing room filled with people; we had opened the interconnecting doors as per the architect's illustration. A few guests drifted into the kitchen; this end of the table where I'm sitting retracts, and we had folded it away and pushed the table against the wall to make more space. The kitchen door flipped shut and open, and the movement caught my eye. I saw the boys and their two friends slip out, each holding a beer.

I do wonder if Mika set that alert properly.

Someone squeezed my arm. I spun around. But it was Samirah, our old neighbour. I'd also asked Malcolm, another former neighbour, and from the library Mika and Pauline and Gerald (but not Susan). Gerald perused my 'short stacks' in the drawing room, which by then had grown into tall stacks, and he and Pauline loitered by them all evening. I showed them, conspiratorially, the Kindle that Kurt had given me for my forty-eighth birthday a few months earlier. My sister Tam came with her boyfriend. From The Close, we had Mick and Andrea, the Frittellis, and Sally and Akhil, who complained incessantly about the resale value of the Marlborough and how they had to keep planing bits off the front door. Salvatore Frittelli bemoaned the arrival of the traffic warden, while Andrea boasted that during her morning stroll to the show home, a bird had shat on her shoulder. However, she did not see the bird, and we all thought if true it must have been flying way overhead. Hilariously, the Glossops came in black tie. As I have said, they have The Close's only other Beaufort, and no doubt it is a misplaced sense of superiority that makes them greet Kurt and me and no other resident. One day I will tell Belle Glossop that although 'cul-de-sac' is always translated as 'bottom of the bag' this is not strictly accurate. I'm afraid the Glossops live in the arse of the sack.

'This is lovely!' Samirah rasped over the music. She complimented all kinds of things: the long counter, the island, the glass 'wall' between the kitchen and garden; though it was October, we had the doors open, and it was lighter in here then, before the house behind got its roof. Samirah envied the garage, the access to it from the kitchen, the soft-close cupboards (no handles: you press the doors to open, and they shut slowly and silently). She said the Beaufort was like a house from a storybook. Thinking about it this week, and having done floor duty in Picture Books, I can only conclude that she meant that it was square, with regular windows, the kind a child might draw. For there is nothing imaginative about the

Beaufort that might earn a place in a storybook: no quirks or frills, just plain corners.

'Maureen's still nosing out her nets,' Samirah said. 'Oh, and I've got new neighbours! Oh, but . . .!' she broke off. 'You knew that! They're in your house! Ha! And they're not even new!'

That was enough of an invite for me. I began to tell her the whole sorry story of the case. I said something stupid like 'My life's life was in that case.' I didn't mean life as in the history of me. I meant that part of me that is at the heart of me. I was talking like a popular song. I *was* a bit drunk. But you see I have always loved singers who make a melancholy tale soar with joy just because the song is coming out, coming out – because you know if they are singing that the pain has given rise to a voice, and a voice that sings freely is never wholly sad. Surely I'm not the only person who finds articulated pain uplifting?

'Please help me,' I said to Samirah. I thought she could knock on her neighbours' door and ask if they had seen my case. As I said, I was drunk. I worried Samirah would find all this absurd, or worse, realise why I had invited her, but she kept a warm smile on her frosted lips, and then to my horror she started to choke. She waved away my offer of water. The whites of her eyes shone. Her chest heaved. And then she began to tell me how her grandmother had given her a shawl when she and – I'm afraid I've forgotten her ex-partner's name – had their first child. 'I tuck it in the pram,' she said. 'Every day I tuck it. One day I come home from the shops. I'm at the front door. Dolen's there. His dummy's there. Shawl's gone.' I tried to picture Samirah's son, but could bring to mind only her daughter, and she I barely recalled because she went to university shortly after we moved in. I guessed the son was older and had already left home.

'Did you find it?'

'I turn around and walk back. I walk carefully over my steps. I'm looking everywhere. I ask in all the shops, not just the ones we went in. We get home very late and my baby is asleep and he's too tired to eat. The next day we go to the library. Not yours, the little one. I'm ages at the photocopy machine. I stick a sign on all the lamp posts, like people stick for cats. My grandmother died not long after she finished that shawl. I want Dolen to have something of her.'

She looked at me expectantly, as if it were my turn to supply something. 'That sounds so stressful,' I said. 'And then what happened?'

She shrugged. 'Nothing happens.'

'What?' I said. What a terrible way to tell a story! She had carried me with her, then cut me loose with no way back. She obviously hadn't looked hard enough for the shawl. That's a mistake I will not make.

I waited for Samirah to acknowledge that all this took place a long time ago and was only a story she sometimes told. But she said nothing. 'And how is Dolen?' I asked.

It had grown very noisy in the kitchen. Samirah raised her

voice. 'He died when he was six. Dropped dead in the playground. He'd be married. I'd be knitting.' She looked up. 'I would have learned to knit.'

'Oh! Oh!' I exclaimed.

Poor Samirah was weeping properly now. Tears rolled down her face, but she made no noise and her expression remained calm. She was like a storm on a windless day. She wiped the back of her hand hard across her nose.

I felt wretched. I put my arms around her as best I could, and as I strained to join my hands that would not join, I felt an inner crumpling, as if I were too thin, too emptied out, to comfort. The ink spot in my head flared and darkly glistened and off dropped its little tail, and I held Samirah like that and I told her I was sorry. I was sorry. I am so very sorry.

'I still look for it,' she said into my ear. 'It's a beautiful shawl.'

———

As we stood apart, I saw what I had failed to see in all the years I had lived beside Samirah. She bore herself in an attitude of grief. She carried the weight of a lifetime, and the weight came from what was not there. How could I have missed it? How grief goes unseen. I looked out to the garden, and saw Tam perched on the arm of the love seat. She gave me a thumbs-up.

Moments later, Malcolm appeared. 'She lost a suitcase when she moved,' Samirah said, nodding at me, and I loved her.

'Just a small case,' I said. 'Brown leather . . .' and off I went again. I won't repeat it here.

Immediately Malcolm began to reminisce about the time he mislaid a camera on holiday in Athens and successfully claimed on his home insurance. I wished I hadn't invited Malcolm. Now my case really was nowhere. He had ejected it from the conversation. At that point, Belle Glossop, who had been listening, asked what was in the case. Luckily, she was interrupted by Sally, who tapped me on the shoulder to say she had counted our kitchen cupboards and we had one fewer than her Marlborough. But as I explained to her, the defining asset of the Beaufort is the huge three-door closet in the hall. And as I have been informed this week, that closet helps the Beaufort to retain its value while the Marlboroughs have become impossible to sell; so many new ones are listed. Our closet is heroic, a lifesaver. Our closet is my golden ticket. Well, of course, that is exactly right. Excuse me a minute. I have had the most wonderful idea.

———

I am going to let Kurt catch me.

In approximately one hour, he will enter the Beaufort through the front door, having collected the car from the station after a day of meetings in London. He will try to walk down the hall. Everything is ready. From the kitchen table, I have a clear view. There is nothing to do but wait.

I cannot help but recall how Kurt flitted busily all night at our party, posting pictures and videos – the new Wendy had a superior camera. He was even happier with it than poor dead Wendy under the cherry tree. He skipped and whistled about the place in a highly patterned shirt, a monochromatic Hawaiian style, which he wore open at the neck. (This was around the time he started to remove his chest hair.) I saw him show Tam, Akhil and then Cousin Richard the video of his talk the month before. All evening people congratulated him. His widgets were in such a promising phase. Every so often he put a glass in my hand and with a serious expression wrapped my fingers around it. We passed each other like that all night, not talking but working as a team. Watching him move alone between all those people, I felt OK about the fact that we were together. I suppose that was the last time I did.

When Cousin Richard reappeared, a good hour after I'd seen him dancing in the lounge with Andrea, he was pretty drunk. Despite this, I insisted on giving him information to interest a policeman. I produced the shark's tooth from my pocket. He looked unconvinced. 'When did you last see this case?' he asked. It was not among our things when we unpacked. Richard nodded, too drunk to be useful. But then he asked, 'Was it worth anything to anyone?'

Why hadn't I thought of that!

I think Richard had been amusing himself up to this point. But he beckoned me closer while Kurt watched from the doorway. 'Ask yourself who had access. A case in your loft can't be reached by anyone, right?' He tapped the side of his nose. 'Inside job,' he said. 'Did you check your old loft? What about your new loft?'

Now, Cousin Richard. I told him he was amazing, and I meant it. Kurt stepped towards us then, snaked an arm around Richard's shoulders and steered him towards his next drink. I watched them go, and for the first time since we arrived in The Close, I felt a joyous sense of possibility, of the box house letting down its walls and opening up around me. I have that feeling again tonight. What I have done to the closet is a sort of scale model of that 'opening up', because right now, dozens of bags for life are strewn across the hall, along with outdoor games the boys liked back when they played outdoors: badminton rackets, sponge balls, bouncy balls, swing balls, both bloody roller skates. The pasta machine and its attachments, detached. The paint tins from when we planned to redecorate are rocking on their sides. I have definitely created chaos. I pop into the Forum to update my acquaintances, and Coryphe replies with a cartoon face of a sly-looking yellow goblin.

I realise that none of this reflects well on Kurt, or me, or how we communicated. I keep thinking that even in Phase One, I must have known it was not really the case I was desperate to find. Because why else did I choose not to confront Kurt? The case – well, it was an obsession. I fixed on it, and nothing could throw me off course.

Kurt has texted to say he will be home in half an hour. To settle myself, I have dropped upstairs to see the boys. I knocked, and both replied when I offered them a drink. From my eldest son's doorway, I glanced at the loft hatch. It was a door to another time, that hatch. I went through it on the night of our party, and afterwards nothing was the same.

That night, their room was thick with smoke and a pungent smell that I did not recognise from a source I could not see. 'What are you four doing?' I said. I tried to figure which invisible speaker was pumping the music. By my feet, a sheet of folded paper held the ends of hand-rolled cigarettes. They had burned holes in the paper, and ash lay in small clumps on the carpet. I could hear the alarm in my voice. But no one answered. They lay sprawled on the beds, limbs tangled. I started to collect the empty beer bottles from the floor, and was shocked to count more than a dozen. I shook my youngest's foot, but he kicked out, a fight-or-flight reflex, and curled into a ball. It was gone midnight. Sleep would do them good, I reasoned. I left them alone, and felt in the cupboard for the pole to the loft.

I opened the hatch and climbed the ladder, a little unsteady in my party shoes. I pulled the cord for the bulb. Near the hatch, the eaves glowed bright, then sloped down into darkness. The attic was hot and smelly, and stuffed to the rafters. I couldn't understand where all these things had come from. Why had we kept heaps of baby equipment when our children were teen-agers? At what point does the meaning drain from things? A spilling sound above my head told me it had begun to rain. The boys' music retreated, subdued by wads of insulation. I moved a crate of teddies, and beneath it was an opaque plastic tub I had never seen.

I unclipped the lid. A knot of black cables wrapped around each other like coiled vines, and when I pulled at a loop, I dredged up twists and tangles that snagged mobiles like bricks, mobiles like small bars of chocolate, ones that slid and ones that flipped, palmtop computers, dated but still shiny, two BlackBerrys, an assortment of styluses – I believe the plural is styli – and right at the bottom, Kurt's little pager.

Oh, it took me straight back to our first date. I see it spinning fatalistically on the table between us in Canopy, that restaurant overlooking the common, and I see mine and Kurt's world turning in there. But at our first dinner, after we'd worked through our huge bowls of pasta – this was in the days before small plates – Kurt flicked that little pager all evening while he asked me about where I grew up and I told him about my dad, how he was a boatbuilder, and my dad's affair, how money was tight, then tighter after they split. He circled the glass rings on the table with his thumb, flipped a beer mat, and twirled his hair, which was fuller then, and curlier. His own dad had died when he was thirteen. When I think of that evening, it is the pager I see revolving, Kurt flicking it restlessly – longing for it to vibrate, no doubt. But I didn't think that at the time. I took his fidgeting as a sign of nerves and I too felt trepidation about the date. I had composed a cancellation email, which I kept revising in the drafts folder of my Lotus Notes.

I left quite a gap between our first and second dates; I had a lot on my mind. But I am certain that if smartphones had been invented, Kurt would have petted his phone all evening, and the next time he asked, I would have told him I was busy. Now Wendy is killing our marriage. Even though in the library I can find no categorical proof that smartphones end marriages, and I have spent a long time looking.

I lobbed the pager back in the box.

I was about to step further into the loft when the boys' music abruptly silenced. Returning to the hatch, I saw Kurt at the foot of the ladder. His eyes widened, lighting the whites. I had forgotten his eyelids could retract that far. Humans are the only animal to show their sclera (as the whites are called), and I gather this is so we can indicate to other humans where our attention lies. Kurt eyeballed the boys, the ladder, me. I recall a clear view of his thinning scalp, the blush creeping up his neck inside his Hawaiian party collar. What right did he have to criticise me? I hissed him shush through the hatch and I saw a drop of my spit land on his trainer. His eyes swept the room, the spit, the pole to the hatch, which I had propped in the corner. He planted both hands on the side rails of the ladder.

He means to climb up, I thought. I thrust the lid on the tub in time to see him lift the bottom rung. He began to fold the lower section as if to put the ladder away. With me inside! I refused to be that person, a modern version of a madwoman locked inside a thermally efficient attic with mineral fibre insulation and a concertina rust-proof ladder. What a worn trope that is! Honestly, it is in these moments that I like to picture myself selecting a hammer from the box of tools in the garage and swinging the blunt end down to meet Wendy's unshatterable screen. I am not alone: how else to explain the hundreds of online tutorials? Some people throw the phone from a balcony, some stamp on it, others wield an axe. I like to picture a hammer. But I shall not go there, nor will I allow Kurt to present me as some sort of unhinged person. No. I have a good mind to write my own book. I'll call it *The Madman in the Garage*. Surely that is a phenomenon? Hang on. *No matches found.* How has the male species got away with that?

Of course, none of these reflections occurred to me at the time. I reversed out of the hatch, pivoted on the top rung and crouched. The smoke had thinned, and I could see my youngest fully curled, all five feet of him, in the foetal position. His slim arms bent protectively into his chest, his right cheek rested childishly on his folded knuckles. I thought of Samirah. Oh, I did. I thought of the lost baby.

I jumped. My left ankle twisted, and my shin slammed into the bedpost. I clutched the post to steady myself. I gasped and removed those stupid shoes. Then I hauled myself to my feet and limped my throbbing shin past Kurt to the bathroom. When I returned, he had shut the hatch and roused the boys. I pressed steaming flannels to their faces. It was how I used to revive them when they were small. My boys did not smell good, but under the flannels their faces glistened innocently. Kurt left me to it, and when the children were sitting, I thrust toothbrushes in their hands, distributed pyjamas and sleeping bags to their two friends. All this time, guests were leaving. I'd hear voices in the hall and in the spare room, where Kurt had dumped people's coats – against my wishes – and I'd dart out to embrace one person or another and wave them off into the rain. Tam and her new boyfriend had checked into a hotel in Windsor, and I would see them the next day; Tam was taking me out for belated birthday cocktails. I hugged Samirah, and she hugged me hard. Cousin Richard was the last to go.

All four boys slept, breathing disparately. I sat on the edge of the near bed and listened to Kurt drop bottle after bottle into bin bags, and I felt the cool, damp air waft upstairs while he lugged the sacks outside. I watched the boys sleep and time seemed to sleep too. My two looked so young with their eyes shut. And when I brushed their cheeks with my lips, dropping kisses between the clusters of pimples, their skin was soft and not so unlike baby skin. I laid my cheek against theirs for long, long minutes. I sang to them a made-up love song. I remember the darkness; the quiet, intermittent clatter of the blind slats in the breeze; the pale cup my palm made while I soothed their beautiful heads till their hair flattened around their skulls; the slight fuzzle of their breathing. I knew that in the morning they would wake and all this would be impossible. They both had fine hair, my hair, and it smoothed to a gleam in the dark. I rubbed my love deep into their scalps, as if applying an anti-ageing cream. I did it in the hope that it would last, and I left it to penetrate over the long night till the next time. I would like the boys one day to understand. It is easier to show children love when they sleep. But the pleasure is undermined by the feeling that it is all happening too late in the day. I could lose them, if I am not careful.

That is Kurt's car I hear turning into The Close. I must hurry.

I opened the boys' window. The sky had completely darkened, the rain stopped. I listened to Kurt bolt the front door, kick his shoes against the unornamental skirting. I heard his socked steps enter the lounge, the puff as the sofa cushions exhaled when he sat. It is amazing how many sounds sisal cannot hide. To me, all those sounds were an invite. I thought, I'll speak to him. I'll tell him what Richard said. I'll ask if he has anything he wants to tell me.

He lay heaped on the sofa, his arms flopped wide. I curled beside him, dropped my cheek to his chest. It felt cool and hard, and I tried not to mind the fact that the famously slim Wendy had got there first. I did want to figure out how to talk to Kurt about my case, openly, about what was in it and how to get it back. But I was so tired, so pained, and tender, and I had tucked the boys in for the first time in a year. I stayed there with my cheek on Kurt's touchscreen, trying not to boil, until eventually the glass too felt warm.

When I finally released myself, I saw that Kurt's eyes were

shut; and they were shut shut. I laid a finger on one lid, and traced the shape of an eye. The party was a turning point for me. Kurt had wronged me. But the wrong bound me to him, and fed this ongoing guilt I have.

Ah, his key turns in the door. I must switch browsers and get to my feet.

Antony wrote in emerald ink, usually on lilac paper. It was romantic, he said, an idea I kept faith with even when it didn't feel true. I sneaked into Oxford on a full grant – a termly cheque (basically a voucher from the bank), which was like a student loan but a permanent gift – while Antony won a place to study geology at Edinburgh. In those days, for a very small sum you could post an envelope one day and it would arrive anywhere in the country the next.

Sometimes his letters ran for pages and pages in his beautiful looping hand. He could be extravagant and declaratory, as when he wrote *I love you, I love you, I love you* across a whole page, and no other word but those three. One of his last letters contained a PS in which he promised that if we ever lost touch, he would seek me out at fifty. 'I want to know what you are like as an old woman. I will come and find you,' he wrote. 'PPS I might be a few years late.' Fifty is not old, of course, but we didn't know that then.

I read every letter with joy and foreboding, because although

I loved to receive them, a part of me reserved the idea that each might be the last. Often a scrap slipped out of the envelope. Sometimes there were things he'd found – a Quant button from the sixties, a decade whose music we loved but which seemed cruelly lost to us, having been born into it but too young to live it; a frond of seaweed he had hand-pressed; a picture of a dress he thought would suit me, torn from his mother's *Vogue* (a sort of luxury style blog which they used to print on very shiny paper). His mother, Brigitte, I only ever saw from a distance. She was a very elegant woman. She doesn't live in the mint-green house any more. I don't know where they are. If you try the number, the line goes dead.

Once, I unfolded the lavender sheets and a sketch of a swan fell out, penned in the same vivid ink as the letter. 'Green Swan,' Antony had scribbled. The letter relayed how he had seen the bird on the beach at Deal during a mid-term visit, up near the boats. It had found its way to the sea, and then walked to shore just below the vast bank of shingle where he sat. He sketched it on its feet, staring at him, with those beak eyes that are not eyes, and the swan, despite being out of its habitat, looked as if it owned the paper. After that, the swan became Antony's signature. He sketched them in all positions. Swans with speech bubbles rising from the depths. Swans with and without a mate. Sometimes he bent the initial S of my name into a beautiful, decorated swan.

But this one, the first, I remember clearly. Its neck curved into half a heart, and it contained – to my mind – the same cryptic message to which I have yet to find the answer. Was I meant to supply the other half, or was this Antony's way of saying that half a heart was all he could offer? Did he mean that his half would suffice, or that my heart – and why did I keep it so hidden? – was not enough. Antony inked that swan in countless shapes, but it always proposed the same questions. It is too much to bear that the letters have gone and he may have gone; all that pain and no trace.

94

Kurt boots an upended roller skate down the hall. The wheels are whirring when he thumps his bag on the kitchen table and walks to where I wait at the island. He puts down his phone, picks it up, puts it down. One hand rests either side ('Guard' position). I can tell he is trying to keep it together from the way he nods repeatedly, the little pulse flickering on his right eyelid, but I don't want him to keep it together. I want him to let go of all the pieces. I want him to give up this stupid pretence. I want him to look at me with his eyes wide open and talk to me with his mouth moving and noise and heat coming out so I can feel the air move. And if none of these things is possible, I want him to feel as lost as I do.

Kurt runs his fingers through his hair; this week's cut has removed the curls and it undulates in thick wiry ridges. He flips the door of a cupboard between his hands. He circles the island, leaving all the doors open, then he does a second circuit, trying to whip each shut. This house is the height of modernity, as I have said. The cupboards will not slam, they are soft-close, and this only makes Kurt madder.

95

He looks around for things to vent. He snatches the lid off the tea caddy and shakes out the tea bags. The mess encourages him. Coffee beans ping over the floor tiles with a plinky rattle. When he reaches for the sugar, I run to stop him. The beans split and skitter beneath my feet. A strong odour of coffee rises from the floor. The white tiles are ghosted with white glitter and Kurt has moved on to the drawers. Tea towels, aprons, napkins – out it all flies. I chase him round the island trying to save the things that are easy to reach. I yell for him to stop. I yell his name, but Kurt keeps going. It's like packing, but without the boxes.

He stops, stoops a moment. He is not stopping. He is casting around for the next missile. One after another, cookbooks land on the floor, or hit the granite island with a thump. I wince to hear the pages splay, the poor spines crack. I know we have reached the end only when I see Kurt consider, and reject, the knife block. He fists his eyes, and lets out a funny noise, a gargled yelp, which is a noise of pain but not one I have heard before. His hands slide down his cheeks to his mouth, where they meet in a prayer position. He faces me across the island. Even though he is not on the phone, Kurt has lowered his eyelids.

It is unclear if he expects me to speak, or if he thinks I will understand what he wishes me to say and therefore speech is unnecessary, or if he despairs because I will never understand. When I changed careers, back when the boys were toddlers, and I finally followed my passion for books, I spent a lot of time silent. Libraries were not then the social hubs they are now. There was none of the noisy tapping of keyboards or attention-seeking ringtones that rile some of our – can I say 'visitors'? So I know I've got this. I can shrink Kurt with silence. I watch him rooted there, facing me with his eyelids down, sort of pious. And then a thin gleam silvers the lashes of his left eye. Under the bright LEDs, the gleam grows, spills down his cheek in a long glistening streak. He squeezes his lids to hold the tears. Soon his whole face shines slippery. He swipes at his cheeks with his sleeves and strides to the front door. This one obliges him, slams flimsily in its frame.

I pick up shards of china. Kurt has left alone his mother's little glass butterfly. The last object standing on any surface, it sparkles with sugar. I run it under the tap; just the splashback in its wings. I lift the tea towels from the island, grainy with sugar, and as I do so, I see Wendy.

I really feel sorry for Kurt now, because he does not know how to be on his own. He does not know where to look if not down. Open skies make his eyeballs ache. I know this because I have seen him rubbing them when he looks at me. I picture him in The Old Gables, nursing a pint and flipping a coaster. He will have realised his mistake before he left The Close. I imagine the moment of discovery; his panic as he wrings each lifeless pocket and realises he is truly alone. He must have been desperate to return to the house, and unable to bear the thought of doing so. Tonight, leaving Wendy is an acceptable cost of escaping me, and that makes me feel very, very alone. We both act as if talking will destroy us, but surely silence will, more slowly, and we will be undone by all the things we leave unsaid. I see myself walking out of The Close to the mini roundabout, where the flags hang sadly, turning north to The Old Gables, spotting Kurt at a table and tenderly handing him Wendy. Where would he look first? Which of us would he be most pleased to see?

I ball up the tea towels with the phone and bundle it all in the washing machine. It takes nearly two hours to get the kitchen straight, and all I hear while I work is the muffled clunk of the phone in the drum. Even in its death throes, Wendy gives no peace, but eyes me accusingly through the bubbles. Sixty is a long cycle. When it ends, I hang out the tea towels and leave Wendy on the island with a note explaining that it got swept up with the washing. I pop into the Forum with a brief update. I text Kurt to say I hope he is OK, before I click, silly me, that he doesn't have his phone. Then I find a bottle of brandy, left over from our party nearly two years ago, and pour a large glass. Well, we are out of tea, coffee, sugar, gin.

I lie in bed, waiting for Kurt.

It fascinates me that there is a specific number of times a person must kill in order to qualify, if you like, as a serial killer. But there is, and the number is three. I'd love to know the criminological explanation for a person who murders twice. Was the second time an accident? Do they tell themselves they gave it their best shot and it's just not the career for them? I guess one hopes that the need passes.

It's long after closing time when Kurt comes home. I don't know where he has been and I don't plan to ask. As soon as he steps into our room, with dead Wendy in his hand, I sit up in bed.

'You're going to have to tell me what happened,' I say. 'You're going to have to tell me where my case is.'

Kurt looks at me in disbelief. But I know I'll never find it. I will have to make him give it up.

Phase Two

One Friday morning in spring last year, I kept myself busy while everyone left the house. The boys, who had recently turned fourteen, caught the bus to school, or wherever they went instead of school. Kurt headed to his desk space for creatives; he had taken the refresh mission as far as it could go and had embarked on a design to facilitate finger-free scrolling. By eight thirty, the only other person in the Beaufort was the builder from the estate team; shrinkage affects all new houses to some degree. I got in the car, cleared a few dirty grey shreds of crab apple blossom from the windscreen and set off towards the old place. Andrea looked up and waved her fork at me as I swung out of the drive; she was on her knee pads, weeding a lamp post and talking to the new couple who had just bought the neighbouring Clarence at a discount we all found painful.

I took the same route that I take here to the library, but I ignored my usual exit. As I passed the parade of shops, Maureen, our old neighbour, emerged from the post office. My hand rose to wave, but I forced it down to the wheel and looked straight ahead. I remember Maureen's bewildered face. Well, that's how I picture it now, but I suppose the bewilderment may have been mine, because I realised in that moment that I did not want to be seen. Four or five months after our housewarming, I had run out of places to search in my world. It was time to look in other people's.

I parked at the wrong end of our old street, the end furthest from our old house, and then I walked with the house at my back. The cherry trees that lined the pavement were festooned with blossom. Their knuckled branches couldn't hold it all, and a mat of pink petals covered the paving. The petals fell on me too, and I let them ride on my shoulders. I passed bushy hedges busy with great tits and blue tits and sparrows. I had never taken much notice of the church at the end of our road, but now I saw that it was a beautiful example of early Victorian architecture with a partially circular nave. It was actually the second most popular of ten things to do in the area (number one being the park). The sun warmed my hair. I observed the colour of each front door I passed. I thought of Samirah's shawl. My eyes strayed to the walls and gutters. Funny how persuasive the most implausible hope can be. Actually, it is not funny.

I reached the other side of the park. The Café Continental was my favourite place to take an unclaimed scrap of time when the boys were small. It had a jaunty striped awning, and the same French family had owned it since the mid 1970s, when the word 'continental' upgraded not only cafés, but breakfasts, diets, quilts. Wrought-iron tables and chairs with elaborate scrollwork spilled onto the street. Inside, the café – coffee shop, you would say now – was decorated with strings of onions and chilli peppers and rattan baskets bearing choice items of produce, all of which were specified on their hefty price tags as French. At the counter, I ordered the daily special, even though I hate cornichons. I wish I didn't feel embarrassed to ask a male server for a plain roll. To make matters worse, when I paid with a five-pound note and some coins, he laughed, apparently amused by the sight of three-dimensional money. I was due a penny change, and I did not know, as Mika has explained, that it is a faux pas to wait for small coins. I felt myself grow old while Philippe scrabbled in the till, and when he finally held out a coin with an amused smirk, I waved it away with a gesture that was far too flamboyant for a penny.

I took my old seat at the window by the communal table. I didn't recognise the song they were playing on the coffee shop sound system, but the melody, mixed with the chatter and hiss and clunk of the coffee machine, felt familiar to me, and I began to tap my foot. I guess it was the sound of other people's happiness. I sat there listening, happy myself. The woman next to me shut her laptop and zipped her outdoor pursuits vest, the sort that Kurt took to wearing in Phase Two. I guess she also worked in tech. She tucked in her chair, turned to me and said goodbye, and I smiled. There was nothing strange in it.

When the waiter brought my coffee and the cornichon special, calling my name as if he knew me, I was excited to see that he was still the same waiter. I beamed at him, expecting him to ask where I'd been. But he set down my saucer with the old smile, as if I had never been away, or he didn't know me.

I watched people pass the window – delivery guys, tapering people with laptop bags, women steering pushchairs with their wrists to free their thumbs. The whole place was bustling – and every single person was oblivious to the fact that I had no business being there. I liked that, and when I finished my coffee, I headed to the park. I walked between the vast old planes with their fantastically broad trunks, along the main avenue beside the lake, and sat on a bench in the sun. The wind bent the fountain and blasted blossom from the trees. If a dandelion counts hours, those old cherries must have clocked years with each gust. The pock-pock from the tennis courts drifted over the hedge while the parakeets shrieked. I watched their citric feathers flit between the lime leaves and imagined how free the first parakeet to escape her cage felt. Two swans swam on the lake. It was idyllic. Swans' eyelids close upwards. That must give a different perspective.

Oh, this is rich!

Kurt has this second emailed to say that his phone, the new one, is not in his pocket and he's cycled all the way back to the Beaufort from his workspace and the phone is not there either. Apparently, it's time I stopped this petty nonsense. Ha! And that accusation doesn't sound petty, does it? Interrupting me at work, while I am supporting Pauline on the information desk. Kurt is paranoid. I mean, I have observed that phone intently since he acquired it three weeks ago, the day after its predecessor went the way of the laundry, and it has scarcely left his hand or the new belt bag that he clips around his waist. There is no parting them. To think that after the washing machine incident I tried to persuade Kurt to live without Wendy for one day so we could reconnect. One day! I am done with that! It is a relief to move on, because I was starting to wonder what my typology would be. I have no obvious pattern. I've kept no souvenirs, nothing weird like that. However, I will not be disposing of any more Wendys. I am stopping at two. Wendy is like Hydra, you see: no matter how fatal the blow, another Wendy will always grow back. No, it is much easier and more practicable to separate from a partner than it is to separate a partner from a telephone. Excuse me one moment while I enable the canned response.

Sorry I can't help.

Now, where was I? Oh yes. My first trip back to South Hill. After the park, I took my time, looped around and walked the length of my old road to the car. I know what you are thinking, but you are wrong. I did not even glance at it. The resistance, as I passed, created the strangest feeling. A heat seemed to rise off the bricks. My feet quickened; slowed when the old place was safely behind me. Just before I reached the car, I saw a gleaming penny on the pavement. It fascinates me how some older ones stay shiny while others tarnish. I guess they have experienced less exposure to negatively charged oxygen atoms than other pennies their age. I put it in my pocket.

When I arrived home, I was singing. A line from the song in the Continental had stuck in my head – doo be do be doo . . .

dadda dum dum – and I kept singing this one line. The boys seemed happy too. I offered them a cup of tea, and they accepted! I listened to their chatter and laughed when they laughed. I called the eldest 'love' when I needed him to budge from the fridge, and he moved. Encouraged, I suggested we spend time together, and because both boys looked anxious, I added: 'Family phone night. Like our old family film night, but we all hang out on the sofa on our phones.' When Kurt returned later that evening, he seemed happy too. He was not on Wendy. He laid it on the island and I tried not to ogle it. I didn't tell any of them where I'd been. Nobody asked. There was nothing to tell.

Talk of the devil, that is Kurt making my phone rattle: he has found Wendy.

Great news!

Powerful love stories, the sort a person never really escapes, often begin with a library book. I like to reflect on this truth as I cast my eyes around our reading room this Wednesday afternoon – at the woman with the candle-making business doing her printing, the job seekers on the computers, people milling the stacks, the man with his head tipped back, snoring, the two students who keep breaking off their reading to kiss, and the guy who busks on the parade who is photocopying his sheet music; Augustus, of course, who waits for us to open each day – and I wonder what might be forged in this room, or unfold in decades to come. The machine that counts footfall with each thunk of the door cannot measure the impact of libraries on our visitors' inner lives. We don't all have a birthright of books, houses full of them. I never owned any till Antony bought me some second hand. But libraries are for borrowers, so we are all equals here. And the truth is, all readers are borrowers.

I practically skip back to the information desk from William Shakespeare with our only edition of *Twelfth Night*. The play is a stranger to me, an oversight that feels grievous today. Books throw long shadows. It doesn't take much, does it? A book passed between hands. Pages casually flicked. Love can arise in a riffle. Mr Darcy and Elizabeth Bennet aroused each other's interest with their reading, and I'm sure her books, like Jane Austen's, were from a circulating library. Did you know that the entire romantic plot of *Brief Encounter* depends upon the heroine's weekly trip to change her library book? Oh, I know everyone remembers the chance meeting at the station café, the speck of grit in her eye (from the express train). But those things come later. If it weren't for the library book, she would never have been at the station in the first place. Sure, coincidence plays a part, but 'coincidence' just means 'to fall upon together', so to my eye there is no love without coincidence. And judging by the library's copy of *Twelfth Night*, I think Shakespeare would agree with me. I've checked it out, you see. I will take it home tonight and torment Kurt with the sight of another book in a plastic jacket.

I intend to study this play very carefully. Apparently Samuel Pepys thought *Twelfth Night* silly. But if that were true, why did he see it three times? It seems to me from my admittedly limited reading that Malvolio *is* the best part in the whole play. Certainly he is the focus for the most illustrious critics. William Hazlitt held him in high regard. Samuel Johnson thought him 'truly comic'. But my favourite appraisal (I say this without having seen a performance) is Charles Lamb's: 'Greatness never seems to desert him.'

Oh dear, dear. Today I am very distractible. Very distractible. Antony. Well now, let me see. That's right. Antony. The Friday after my first trip to South Hill, I parked in the same spot at the wrong end of the road and again I made my way to the coffee shop. I waved my new bank card for a latte and pastry and took my usual seat beside the noticeboard. I had recently launched our events programme to try to raise money, or generate income, I should say, and I made a mental note to bring in a poster. Tucked beneath a leaflet for angry yoga was an advert for a play at the local touring theatre. The printing was faded; the dates of the show – a Chekhov, I think – had passed months earlier. The cast were pictured in costume, the women looking glum in long skirts; but the man in the waistcoat caught my eye. I unpinned the flyer. His face was the size of my fingernail and he appeared to gaze directly at me. But when I lifted the image closer to my eyes, his expression, hairline, cheekbones dissolved into dozens of grey dots.

I have no idea what Antony looks like now. Of course, I am familiar with the ubiquitous black-and-white photograph, the one that any internet search would uncover, his hair brushed into a lustrous sweep. But the picture is so old. His profile on the agent's website is still awaiting image. Who knows if he even has hair? The digital age has left his privacy remarkably intact. It is infuriating, but I cannot conjure him at all, bald or not, and the attempt feels uncannily like communing with him.

However, one part of Antony I *can* summon. Have I

mentioned that his parents owned a beach hut on the edge of Deal? It was a premium hut, being large and close to the public conveniences. Antony's mother had furnished it with a futon, and he and I spent many nights there during our summer holidays. I can't recall the exact occasion – what we talked about or how we passed the time. I remember only that it was night. The darkness of the sky, a long way from the last lamp posts, seemed to fold into itself the crunch of the shingle and wash of the sea. When I realised that Antony had fallen asleep, I had the idea that I would keep my own eyes open. I would stay awake and observe him, take in everything I could from this tiny place in a bed of sorts beneath a continental quilt. There must have been a good moon, because I had light enough to see. I remember the picture of Antony's windswept father water-skiing, hung beside the first aid box, the movement of Antony's ribs, my staring, the staying awake, the conviction, though I couldn't have been more than twenty, that this back, speckly with moles and freckles, and tanned from all the swimming, must be committed to memory.

I put the flyer back on the coffee shop noticeboard. Behind me, at the communal table, a young couple were debating a performance they had seen the night before. I tried to work out which play they were talking about, although the play itself interested me less than the way they discussed it. Such a passionate exchange! The woman, Katarina – her name was scrawled on her paper cup – was irritated by a gesture that one of the actors had overused. I turned towards the communal table. Katarina held out her hands in the shape of a goblet, her fingers a stiffly curved bowl, her wrists and forearms the stem. The man leaned across the table with his own goblet hands. But he disagreed with her. He liked the gesture. He called it 'the chalice'; it was a vessel for offering and acceptance, he said. He may have said, or I may have thought, that belonging to any audience is a highly creative act. Katarina was a little verbose, but neither she nor her partner seemed to mind how long each took to say things. I know the boys would like to speed me up. They like everything at 1.5. On and on these two went. Her then him then her then him, she eventually bashing his goblet with hers in glee, before they leaned across the table and got off with each other. Is it still all right to say that? Is making out better? Smooching? I know that in France they do not call it French kissing.

I am still in the library, by the way, reading historical reviews as I attempt to piece together the ultimate Malvolio. We shut our doors to the public an hour ago, Augustus the last visitor to go as usual, at the same time as my co-workers. But tonight I am finding it hard to leave. Some extremely fine actors have played Malvolio. John Gielgud, Laurence Olivier, Derek Jacobi . . . In terms of prestige, I have read that it is close to Hamlet. A wonderful role. An accolade. I wish I could discuss this with someone. I think that's what I envied those young people in the coffee shop last year. They picked over their sayings with immense care. They really paid attention, separated and tweezered each other's words, and I tried to think of a time when Kurt and I had done that, when one of us had said something and the other had replied in a way that incited further reply, creating the effect of what we once would have called a conversation.

I visited South Hill every Friday. I parked in the same spot at the wrong end of the road. In fact, I parked there so often, it began to feel like the right end of the road. I came to regard the journey from the Beaufort to our old house as my new commute. I felt I was driving from an 'after' to a 'before', back to a happier place, or was it a happier time? I could sense my little lost case just by being there, as if it were close at hand, calling to me, and I would find it if I kept walking. My bare feet pad up and down now on the cool lid of the trunk Kurt bought me. With its ornate claret and gold lining it really does resemble a well-dressed theatre; I cannot resist thinking of the theatre again. But what will play out in there?

———

Antony wrote in fits. Some months several letters arrived, then nothing for weeks. A couple of times a term he would write and tell me he was coming to see me, and I would get everything ready – by which I mean I would buy the second cheapest bottle of wine in the off-licence and shave my legs – then wait to see if his person would bear out his letter. Antony liked to write. He was very romantic, but he was not always a man of his word. Letter after letter I slipped into my leather case, which sat on the hearth by the three-bar heater. Antony didn't notice. I could have kept a pet elephant and he wouldn't have noticed; he was so busy with the things in his head. He would rattle off this and that, zip us along to some play – he was the visitor, but he always knew better than I where to go, he must have read it in some paper newspaper, or someone else's posted letter, because how else did we find things out? I listened so hard. How I listened. I hung on his words.

———

In the Continental, there was always something going on. Who needs a mobile phone? One morning I sat and watched an articulated lorry reverse around the corner. Not once did the waiter raise an eyebrow at me. I grew to find his lack of excitability reassuring. I had become a regular. I was dependable, regular in the purest sense: I was there at the same time every week. This may seem absurd, but it made the whole enterprise feel less, well, irregular.

I began to settle back into the neighbourhood. Yes, we had lived there for more than ten years: what was to settle? But returning to a place can make a person feel more at home, or less. Shortly before we moved in together, Kurt and I went to Oxford on a mini break (as we called weekends). We strolled the quads and cobbled streets and meadows down to the river. We behaved like tourists. Well, Kurt did, and I was his guide. I remember he wanted to try rowing. We stayed in a beautiful Renaissance courtyard in my old college, and Kurt enjoyed the privilege of it, which was a funny feeling for me, because I felt I counted for something in that setting. And I felt proud, as one feels proud of a place one used to call one's own – but also fearfully estranged, because it was my place no more and, given the full grant and so on, it was obvious from a distance how little it had ever truly been mine. I certainly never dreamed of rowing. I didn't try to explain any of this to Kurt. I could share the beautiful place, but the estrangement was all mine.

My visits to South Hill weren't like that. I walked for hours in a state of joyful comfort, and shopped like a local. One Friday, I bought a pair of plimsolls on the parade. 'Look, Mum's got herself some sneakers,' one of the boys said. They drew a blank at the word 'plimsoll', and claimed, implausibly, never to have heard it. Another Friday, walking through the park, I recognised a parent from the boys' old school; mother of Yusef. She stopped in front of me, with a beautiful little girl in the buggy, and the little girl looked just like her. I was thirty-five when I had my two – two at once – so a girl was impossible. Yusef's mother asked after the boys, how they were coping with their pre-mocks, or was it pre-pre-mocks? She was the first person to notice me. Until that moment, nobody's eyes seemed to catch on me. But Yusef's mother's did. She pushed me into the open, and I felt the responsibility of being visible. This time, when I reached the house, I did not walk past.

Our jolly red door was now a dull and no doubt classy grey. That was one thing. My hedge – that was a surprise. It was doing rather well. It looked . . . happier. I absent-mindedly fingered a leaf that had sprung through the railings, large and smooth and glossy. The new people had fitted those repro shutters, which made the windows look simultaneously more and less original; I felt a twinge of guilt for the plum brocade. Then I saw that they had changed the house number.

I mean, it was the same number. But our little brass 71 had gone, and a huge SEVENTY-ONE was printed in block capitals on the glass above the door. Why would anyone do that? It would always be 71, so just leave it. Four small black holes in the door told where the screws that had fixed my old numbers had been, and which the new people had tried to fill with grey paint.

I rang the bell. I eyed Maureen's curtains next door. I dreaded being seen.

Samirah did shifts; she would be at work or asleep. What about Malcolm? But don't worry. No one answered. I waited on our old step and I pictured Kurt in the doorway, his grey eyes smiling at me, and the boys careering into the hall when they heard my bicycle bell, flinging open the door so enthusiastically I worried for its hinges. And I saw Kurt edging through the door sideways, his arms awkwardly crooked, a car seat in each hand, with our babies, the evening we brought them home from hospital. I saw the years of thinking: Maybe another. I stood on the step for a few minutes, but I walked away with the sensation that a lifetime had passed.

It was a strange drive home. Our old, tight corner of London gave way to wider roads, then fields, the odd horse, and just before I hit proper countryside, I turned off the motorway. Of course I did. I do this drive every day after work. I have just done it today. The sun – if it is sunny – hits me always on the same bend, and on this day the light streamed over the dusty wind-screen. The road unravelling before me jumped with a silvery haze. I was only twenty minutes from home, but I didn't feel I was nearing home. I felt home was further and further behind me and the Beaufort was a sort of waiting place in obvious decline. Quicker than the builder filled the cracks between the walls and the woodwork, more black lines jagged the paintwork, and the rooms were pockmarked with popped nails.

The boys came in singly. Kurt arrived in his sustainable gilet, scrolling. He did his ritual fiddle with the thermostat. If new houses get hot, the cracks grow. I thought his eyelids looked paler than normal. I said hello. Hello, hello. Then I gave up. In our house, Kurt is what the boys call an NPC, a sort of non-player character. Not for the first time, I thought, There are three of us in this marriage. But why stop at three? Why not count his two laptops, the big tablet, the small tablet and the TVs? The house phone rang and none of us moved to answer.

I wanted air, so I thought to walk the rim. Stepping outside,

I saw a small crowd in the road. Andrea greeted me with a note of reproval. A tyre mark had appeared in The Close – a thick black streak like a scaly tail, printed on the ivory road directly outside our house – and did I know how it had got there? Belle Glossop said she had an idea. She mentioned the graffiti of the show home; we had all received a notice through the door asking us to be vigilant. Akhil squatted. He dabbed at the streak with his finger. Mick came out with a scrubbing brush and a bowl of soapy water. I refuse to believe that a tyre mark is a sign of a person unravelling. Surely anyone who thinks that needs to let out their own ravel. Besides, couldn't any of them see that all the roads were grubby now? I strode to the mini roundabout, where the flags hung ragged and streaked with dirt, and I kept going. It took ten minutes to reach the orange barriers. The foundations of Phase Two had long since been laid where the fields once were, and the first townhouses of the Cultural Quarter were complete. I looked for the sunset. Several evenings over the following weeks I looked. The boys say the estate is like a 1980s maze game, and I walked every road I could find. I walked and walked, to The Old Gables, which looked finished but was not yet open, and well beyond the show home, but in every direction my walk ended at a run of orange barriers. The estate had lost the sunset. And what was worse, I didn't even see it go.

There came a Friday when it rained heavily in South Hill, one of those drenching June showers. I took my time in the coffee shop, happy to be wrapped inside its misted windows. When I could eke out my pastry no more, I browsed the shops and estate agents on the parade. I sheltered under the awnings while rain poured onto the pavement. I visited the local library – not mine, the little one, where Samirah had photocopied her posters – and I took out three books, one each for the boys and me. This was an act of solidarity more than leisure, because the council had announced the closure of the little library. We worried, all of us, for our futures. I went in and out the door several times, just to increase the footfall.

In the post office, quaint enough to sell paper by the leaf, I bought a pale blue sheet of 'Conqueror'. It seemed a grand claim for a piece of paper, but I admired its confidence, more so when I learned it was the brainchild of an enterprising Victorian who wanted to make high-quality writing paper for the masses. I handed over ten pence for the sheet, fifteen for the matching envelope and a small fortune for the postage stamp, then I took my purchases to the coffee shop, a few hundred steps away, ordered another coffee, and wrote to the people who had bought our house to ask if they had seen my case. I suggested some places it might be. I mentioned the loft. I thought it would look creepy to hand-deliver it, so I addressed it to *The Occupiers* and put it in the postbox.

———

I could have gone on quite happily like that.

Then one Wednesday evening in late summer I got back from a drink with Mika to find a letter at the Beaufort. It was from Zoe Porter, the woman who had bought our house. She thanked me for getting in touch. It was nice to hear from me; a surprise, nearly two years after they had moved. She thought I'd like to know that she and her partner were very happy in the house. The house was well loved. She also said that she was very sorry but she was unable to help with my case.

You can see the problems that thrive in the space that words leave. 'Unable to help'! When there were so many things she could have said. Such as, we searched the loft as you suggested. We checked the built-in wardrobes and the cupboard under the stairs. She actually made no mention of the loft, even though I had explicitly said it was the likeliest place. Zoe Porter had not truly looked. She had not looked as I would have looked.

I felt so fobbed off. Three months passed before I had any desire to drop by the old place again. I went into work, came back here to the Beaufort. Not here exactly, as we have had to vacate for the day. We have all gone 'out': the boys, as they do most Saturdays, to the mall. Kurt no doubt to his workspace for creatives. I too am taking refuge in the mall, grateful for air conditioning. I found the boys a nice T-shirt each in the last of the summer sales, then I came and sat at one of these little tables outside a coffee shop. Half an hour ago they walked past with a couple of friends from school, and my youngest waved. My eldest did not look at me, but at least I know where he is. This place is a chain, of course, nothing like the Continental.

―――

When I eventually drove back to South Hill, it was shortly before last Christmas. Kurt was jaded and aloof. From what I overheard, his scrolling innovation had stalled. He needed more funding, but every lead seemed to leave him at the same impasse. The bookshelves he had promised to put up for me in the drawing room took weeks to reach the ceiling, partly because new cracks continued to surface in the walls, despite Kurt's rigorous ventilation schedule. But he did finish the shelves, and I was grateful, and I agreed that once they were full I would acquire no more physical books. Occasionally in the evenings we'd abandon our separate prongs and sit side by side; yes, even in Phase Two. Not speaking, our arms shaping a rickety bridge between us while we let the TV play. Sometimes Kurt thumbed the back of my hand: a substitute for scrolling, I suppose, a sort of phone replacement therapy. He has stopped doing that.

One night, seated like this, I tried again to talk to him. I wanted to tell him I had been going to South Hill on Fridays, because although I'd gone there looking for my ancient case full of prehistoric letters that I wasn't fussed to read (it was really the lucky stone I wanted), I'd found all kinds of other things. I wanted to tell him the hedge was thriving. That the Continental had a new awning. And about the silly house number. That I'd found a kind of peace. So I said, I went to South Hill today. I dared not look. When Kurt said nothing, I took a full, slow breath as I do at yoga, and I said, I've been going there on occasional Fridays. (No need to be exact.) Sometimes I drop by at lunch.

Kurt cleared his throat. I looked at him. The whiteheads on his eyelid had yellowed and were hard as barnacles. They were not as bad as Casaubon's moles. He did not turn to me. As you know, we have problems with our face-to-face interface.

I went to South Hill today, I said again, louder this time.

Kurt's right eyelid pulsed in reply, but his mouth emitted no sound. Not responding, you see. He really did privatise his auditory space to an incredible extent. Come on, I said, it's only a three-minute listen! Think of it as a chance to verify your humanity. I said, today I slept with someone in the quiet room. (This was fictitious.)

I'm in love with someone else.

Shall we get takeaway?

While I sat beside Kurt waiting for him to reply, to take a break from counting his pixels or simply to exhale audibly, to cause any vibration of air to signal that he had heard me, I became aware of a development that made me smile. Yes, the silence between us was deepening and spreading. But I felt my power grow. I held my head still. I did not want to move and break Kurt's concentration, because he had let his chance pass. I thought, I might save him from that pitiable absorption, and I don't want to save him. I want him to face the consequences. Instead of waiting for him to speak, I began to see that I could nurture the silence. I could let it grow, and find my own space within it. I scorn Kurt's absorption, which makes me absent to him even when I sit beside him with my hand on his leg. You see, if I'd broken his trance, I'd have lost my proof. But he kept looking at his phone, so the proof is here. I have it, and you have it. Kurt cannot hear me. He lives his life behind glass.

After five minutes, I stood calmly from the sofa, lest I draw attention to my departure and thereby invest it with an emotional significance such as frustration or bitterness or despair or rage, from which Kurt might derive the satisfaction of having communicated.

I stopped waiting for Kurt and I started to act.

I sat at my desk in the drawing room. I opened a new tab and typed into the search engine:

Where's my leather case

Why does my partner prefer his mobile to me (This is how I found the Forum.)

Is Antony alive

What must I do to make Kurt give me back my case

There is no need for question marks, is there. They have been widely dispensed with, as Mika has pointed out in this week's bulletin. And there is no need ever to be lost for an answer. All you have to do is key in and enter, key in and enter. And the next day, that's exactly what I did.

I rang the doorbell as usual.

I knew no one would answer. They were never home when I called. In a funny way, with me going there on my days off, which had begun to feel like days on, we shared the house. I was careful not to intrude. I was never there at weekends, and they were never there on Fridays. While I was thinking this – standing on the doorstep in the usual unexpectant distraction – my hand dipped into my bag for my keys.

To my surprise, the door opened.

I should have pulled it shut and hurried to my car at the end of the road. But I was so shocked to feel it give with its old ease, I stepped into the hall. Zoe Porter, a person organised enough to reply to the letters of strangers, had neglected to change the locks – because who moves and doesn't think to change the locks? Other than those who buy numbered plots on new estates.

Zoe Porter's hallway was thick with hanging coats and macs. I had the feeling I was hiding inside a wardrobe. I stood rooted to the doormat, and when I looked down to check that my

127

shoes hadn't brought in any telltale autumn leaves, my fate was sealed, for the mat was printed with the words *Come In!* I was overwhelmed by the sense that Zoe Porter and her partner had been expecting me. I realise this is silly, by the way. I'm just trying to explain why I didn't walk straight out. The house had an intentionally welcoming vibe. Below the coats, a narrow wayfarer's bench was pushed against the wall. This struck me as an odd spot to offer visitors a seat, but I sat down. I gave myself a moment to get used to the sensation of being there. A long rug stretched down the hall, uncluttered by enormous teenage sneakers. I followed it into the house.

The place smelled unlike home. I guessed Zoe Porter and her partner cooked different food, washed their clothes, their bodies, with different soap and had stuck their expensive new paper to the wall with different glue. I checked my watch. I had an hour. That was plenty. I would not pry. I would hunt for my case and leave.

Zoe Porter had squeezed two sofas into the lounge: one dove grey, the second a rich, velvety fuchsia. I admit, I felt jealous. I will have a bright couch in my next lounge. I have gone off L-shaped sofas. Perpendicularity is not always what one wants from one's intimates. In an alcove beside the chimney breast, Zoe Porter had placed a small desk, smaller than this one of mine. Box files lined one shelf, and the desk itself was tidy: a paperweight, a low pile of papers. I had absolutely no interest in the papers. It was a cursory glance, the sort that had become habitual in two phases of searching, that made me pause.

A pale blue triangle of Conqueror peeped from the sheaf of papers. I pincered the corner and whipped it from the stack. Honestly, I touched none of Zoe Porter's papers. I touched only my letter. I scanned the first side.

As a rule, I like to tweak and rewrite everything, even emails before I send them; and afterwards I like to reread what I wrote in my sent box. Nothing strange in that. No document composed on a computer or tablet or on the mobile internet is static, is it? They all exist in a sort of perpetually updatable, adjustable and rewritable present. But it is a different experience entirely to come across your own unalterable bare hand in someone else's house. I groaned aloud as I read. I winced at the overly fawning and solicitous tone. I don't know why I have never learned to ask for things without sounding so damned apologetic. Really, I could have got away with explaining a lot less. In one corner of my letter, there was a large blue tick, beneath which Zoe Porter – I recognised her writing – had scribbled 'Replied 10/08'. I turned the letter to read the reverse, and my arms sank with the weight of the page: beneath my signature, in a different pen, were the words 'NUT JOB!!!'

At the time, as I have endeavoured to explain, I was in a difficult place. I was trying to cope with everything that had changed since we moved, trying to relocate myself and something I held dear. And of course I approached that task single-mindedly. It maddens me that social norms make us see a person with an intense and specific desire as deviant, unless the passion is deemed cool, in which case the person is an 'outlier'. (I'm aware that no one who says 'deemed' will ever be cool.) I felt so alone. I ached for the Forum, but they were shut up inside my phone. Life was all the harder because I was aware of Kurt's – and now Zoe Porter's partner's – opprobrium. Her partner must have read my letter first, then passed it to Zoe Porter for reply. Or maybe he had left it out with this little comment for her to laugh at, and she, being kinder, had found time to respond. I wanted to take my letter home with me, but I had no business being there, so I replaced it in Zoe Porter's pile.

I felt demoralised. I craved a cup of tea, and might have made one in Zoe Porter's sleekly refurbished kitchen with uncracked walls if I weren't scared that someone would return to find the kettle warm. I supposed that at some point Zoe Porter and her partner *did* come home. The house felt lived in, just – not much. Anyway, I had a job to do. I unlatched the cupboard under the stairs and switched on the light. Every container on the shelves was clearly labelled. There was no provision for random forgotten things. There was nothing they had outgrown but kept.

When I was pregnant, we emptied the study in Zoe Porter's house to make space for the boys. Kurt put my little old case and his shoeboxes of bank statements under the spare bed. (This was in the days before domestic shredders.) Over the years, my old leather case enjoyed many homes – the bottom of the wardrobe, the cupboard under the stairs, and eventually it found its way to the attic. That was fine. Old love letters are meant to collect dust; I'm sure Malvolio would agree. And this reminds me: I must book a day off next week to confront our loft. Occasionally, after the boys were born, when Kurt would haul up to the attic the things we were done with – the cribs and the double buggy and the car seats, the boxes of teeny-tiny clothes, of small clothes, and then quite amazingly large clothes – he would ask if I still wanted the case. The loft was filling up. But I would have put out almost anything before that.

———

In all those years in South Hill, I never read Antony's letters. Honestly, I never felt the need. They lived in the house, and I lived alongside them. Why was I able to let Antony go for all those years, but not now? Did I let him go? I suppose the letters meant he was still there, in his own special not-there way, and that was how I had always learned to live with him. At what point does a gone thing become irretrievable? For what it's worth, I think loss becomes finite only when you give up hope. The wonder of hope is that it can outlive probability by many years.

I doubt these thoughts occurred to me as I stood in Zoe Porter's study. I disliked the feeling of being in someone else's house. The only thing that made it all right was the sensation that in a faint, residual way, their house was also my house. And that too is ridiculous, because the prices on our old street have rocketed. Even a three-bedroom flat is unaffordable.

I knew I had to move fast. In Zoe Porter's bedroom, the blinds were open, and anyone watching from the other side of the street could see me, could see I was the thing that I'd left behind. Although I had a sense of belonging, I felt trapped between this feeling and the conflicting sense that I was trespassing. I know what you are thinking. I *was* trespassing. But bear in mind that back then I felt I was trespassing every minute. On this house, on the boys' affection, on Kurt's attention – I felt so thoroughly disinvited in every department of my life that even in Zoe Porter's bedroom, my discomfort was no greater than the unease I felt in my own home. Besides, I was there. I had done the hard part. I got on with the looking.

The case was not under the spare bed, just woolly clumps of dust and a cratered exercise mat. I was looking in the built-in wardrobe for the pole to open the loft when I heard a key in the front door. The key went back and forth.

I dived under the spare bed. Do not laugh. What else could I do? I lay on my stomach. My heart drummed like knuckles on the wooden boards. Knock knock, knock knock. Those words beat in my head as I heard Zoe Porter step into the hall.

I wriggled further beneath the bed. I pointed my toes so I did not stub or squeak my sneakers. Each slight movement made my shirt buttons clink on the floorboards. I heard Zoe Porter step into the kitchen. She turned on the tap. A cupboard door slammed; they had not got the soft-close. Above me, the heaviness of the bed pressed on my head and gave me the feeling that I was being pushed down through several storeys of my life, a quick drop down the shaft. What a mess. I began to think of Antony. Oh, I did!

I shut my eyes and Antony's tongue entered my mouth. The possession and obliteration. The ink spot in my head smudged and bulged like a kidney bean, and began to wiggle. Since that first kiss on the shingle beach, after the theatre in Margate, Antony seemed to know his way around. He wiped the back of my teeth. He rolled my tongue. Sucked my lip. Searched about in there while the seagulls cried. That one tongue could do all this! He slipped his knee between my knees, and as we shifted, the pebbles crunched and jangled, disputing all our subtlety. And under Zoe Porter's bed, I forgot my predicament because there was Antony's tongue in my mouth, hot and vivid and such a muscular memory that I swear I felt so close to him, the hum of his body, the bundled-up musk of his clothes, seemingly unearthed from mussed sheets, the saltiness of his shoulders. We kissed till our lips swelled and our mouths bloomed raw red rims.

Squashed by the slats of Zoe Porter's spare bed, I had the feeling that I had climbed inside my case. The wooden bed above my head was the lid. I tried to turn my neck, but the bed was too low, and of course Antony wasn't there: only the clumps of dust. It amazes me that someone has thought to name them dust bunnies. Then I heard feet on the stairs. Heavy feet. For the first time, it occurred to me that the other person in the house might be Zoe Porter's partner.

The footsteps entered the bathroom at the far end of the

landing. I recognised the elastic snap of our old light cord. I did not hear the bathroom door close. I wondered what he was planning to do in there, and how long it would take him. I began to slide toward the edge of the bed, dragging myself sideways with firm, flat hands. I was desperate to get my head out from under there. The feeling of compression, of something being squeezed out that really should stay in . . . At last I knelt on the floor beside the bed. I gave myself a moment to recover, brushed the dust bunnies from my clothes. I turned to take one last look at where Antony had been. From the bathroom, a mobile phone rang to the tune of 'La Bamba'.

Before I could gather my thoughts, the person in the bathroom began to speak loudly and quickly in – I'm guessing – Spanish. I peeped along the landing. The woman I saw leaning over the bath, scrubbing with one hand and waggling the shower hose with the other, had dark hair twisted into a bushy plait. A cord dangled from her ear, and she was chatting into a mouthpiece. I felt the fear go out of me. The woman in the bathroom was not Zoe Porter but Zoe Porter's cleaner. While she bent over the bath, her words and the water running into the plughole, I slipped downstairs.

I drew the door quietly behind me, and as soon as I was on the pavement, I vowed never to enter that house again, and I meant it. I was so glad to reach my car in its bay at the end of the road.

So now let's see.

I have: a torch, a roll of bin bags, three sheets of large sticky labels and a couple of permanent markers borrowed from the library, a bottle of water, a plain cheese sandwich and some trail mix. I have seven hours alone in the Beaufort's loft, and I am not going back down that ladder till I have scoured every box, every laundry bag, every random-shaped container containing random-shaped bits of our lives, till I can say with absolute certainty that my case is not in this house. I cannot see myself ever leaving this place if I have not done this. But what a mess! I will start at the front and work back.

———

It is lunchtime when I reach the ladder again.

I knot my jumper at my waist and dangle my legs through the hatch. It is cooler than last week but still warm for early

September. While I eat my sandwich, I survey my progress. I am leaving my secret overspill bookcase full for now, but I have emptied my old college and university papers into sacks for recycling. There is a whole folder devoted to *The Portrait of a Lady*, and I cannot understand what I meant by most of it. I have boxed countless knick-knacks from my flat in Finsbury Park, where I lived when I dated Kurt. I'm unsure if this stuff is rubbish or ephemera. I found the staff card for my first assistant librarian job, and my old lacquered pop-up telephone index. Under 'Antony', my younger hand has written two numbers: one for the mint-green house in Deal, the other for a hotel in Bloomsbury.

I glug the bottle of water and knock back the trail mix, eyeing the plastic tub of Kurt's old tech. Beneath it sits a much larger crate, industrial-looking, which contains his old gaming gear: cartridges, joysticks, and a beige and brown keyboard that says 'Commodore', model number 64, which even I have heard of. Some prototypes that look home-made and don't mean much to me. I sit the smaller plastic tub, the one I found during our housewarming, on my lap. I am looking, of course, for the little blue pager.

———

It feels very affecting to hold it.

I place it on the boarded floor of the loft and flick it gently. So much of the past eighteen years seems to turn in that flick.

I have gone from my thirties to fifty, a young woman to . . . not yet an old one; but I left something of myself behind back there. I see now that my first date with Kurt was a time of great possibility for me, when I had choices, when I was the person spinning the wheel. I did not know it then, in those few weeks when everything happened to me. I felt that I was on the receiving end of my life, and I did not appreciate that I was a person who also made things happen; that mine too was the power to act.

The ladder creaks. My eldest is home and he looks really fully grown, almost a man, the shadow of a moustache on his upper lip. He wants to know what his mother is doing in the loft, and whether she has been at large in his room all day. He helps me with the bags and boxes, going up and down the steps. Then my youngest appears, and he does look younger, by much more than a minute. He joins us and we all three carry the things out to the car while Andrea watches from her front garden. We fill it until there is room only for me, my bag and Kurt's tub of old phones.

For the first time ever, I have to wait at the mini roundabout for a succession of cars; some kind of party in the Cultural Quarter. I drive to the dump.

I did take Kurt's plastic tub of old tech. I snapped it at the dump with the skips in the background, then I popped into the Forum with the picture. Coryphe replied immediately. 'You go girl!' I wonder how old Coryphe is. I wonder how old Coryphe thinks I am. But I have brought the tub home again. I am thinking about that. In the meantime, I have locked its contents inside my new burgundy trunk, on top of some of these pages. I print them out every few days. It is filling up in there, and I get the feeling this lavishly marbled interior will finally house a performance.

It was not in the loft, incidentally. My case. It did occur to me that the letters may have been hidden singly. But I have checked the backs of mirrors and paintings, and inspected the hollow table legs for signs of disturbance. The letters are not in the Beaufort.

After I entered our old house, the week passed in a kind of elation. Instead of feeling sheepish, or diminished by my transgression, I drove to the library each day with renewed vigour. I threw myself into work. I caught up with acquisitions, and I revamped Geology, which had become terribly neglected. The codes were all out of sync. I put two people on the self-service kiosk, to try to soothe our – customers. That is what we are to call them now. And I organised a little party for Gerald, to celebrate his forty years at our library; and I tasked him with expanding our self-service provision. He was thrilled, as he had taken it personally when the reference library had shrunk to two small bays. He had no wish to retire and said he would not know where else to go.

But when I thought about what had happened in Zoe Porter's house, I felt perplexed. Was I happy because I had got away with it? Because I had put one over on Zoe Porter and her partner and their cleaner? I don't think so. I warmed to Zoe Porter and her perky decor. I found more of myself in her house than

I was able to find in my own. This happiness underlay all that I did. I knew that something good was waiting for me. I felt myself draw closer to it. In the new year – I mean, of course, in January this year – I reverted to my old routine. I went to the park, browsed the parade, the estate agents. I sat in the coffee shop and penned an introduction for an event I'd organised with an eminent memoirist. The closure of the little library had been postponed – though sadly it looms again. To support it, I continued my habit of borrowing books for the boys. It was what we used to do, the three of us, when they were small, and I liked to stand there and try to work out what they would pick. I withdrew, and read, a book on Steve Jobs, who Kurt once loved to talk about, and who I gather from the newspaper websites is seriously ill. I never gave my two the books I chose for them. They wouldn't have wanted them. That was OK. I was happy doing what I was doing. I took books out, took them back, and that little routine helped me to feel close to the boys. When I'd completed my jobs, as I thought of them, I sat at the bus stop and watched the house. Someone had stuck a mitten on our old railings, and it seemed to wave at me. There was no reappearance of the cleaner. Friday was not her regular day.

In practical terms, this explains why late in Phase Two, this would be in April, I again let myself into the house. These thoughts sound crazy written. But I believe a crazy thought is a close neighbour to a sensible one. They share a hinge; slight pressure can cause a movement either way. So please don't see me, as Kurt does, as deranged or out of control. I know from the library that ordinary people can do all kinds of extraordinary things. A woman can stand and lift her arms and sing in a room full of silent people, and other people will look up and look down and some will shush and life will go on. And that happened in the reading room again yesterday, by the way. I have told my co-workers: let the woman sing. Her name is Edna.

In Zoe Porter's hall, there were fewer coats and shoes; a change I put down to the fine spring weather. This time I did not sit on the wayfarer's bench, which was partially obstructed by a large hard-shell suitcase. I went straight up to lie on the spare bed. I wanted the memory I found last time to come again. I had tracked down something better than my case, something I believed was inside. I lay still, careful not to dirty the throw with my sneakers. But alas, the strong feelings from my previous visit did not return. Maybe because I was *on* the bed, or because I had dared to hope for them, or because these things don't happen twice. Every time I caught up with Antony, he gave me the slip.

Kurt, I say. Kurt.

Love, could you put that down, please? Can we talk?

There is something I've wanted to say to Kurt since I cleared the loft last week.

His near eyelid twitches. He has heard me. Kurt is a formidable multitasker, but I am one task too multi.

While he thinks about it, I'll carry on here. It suits us both that I am busy. I shall just get rid of all these browsers that overwhelm my screen. Farewell to the confirmation of my purchase of a statement necklace I can ill afford from a luxury retailer, reviews of Gateshead hotels, an article on the typology of pragmatic mission-oriented serial killers, and that silly picture of Antony with his flicked fringe.

I am letting myself get distracted again. I was saying that it felt incredibly exposing, and lonely, to lie there on Zoe Porter's spare bed. You will understand how piteous I felt if I say that it was relief, not fear, that rinsed through me when I heard the key in the front door.

This time the footsteps were brisk. Quick, light heels clipped the tiles in the kitchen. I got to my feet. I stood in the spare room, looking at the bed, its rumpled throw, and listening to the movements below. Antony hadn't come, but Zoe Porter had. There she was, running the tap, clapping the lid of the kettle. I looked at my watch. I felt trapped, boxed in, and – I confess – a little irritated to be reduced to hiding in my own spare room, as was. Why had Zoe Porter come home in the middle of the afternoon? I reached into my bag, checked the time, switched to silent. I'd promised to collect the boys from a friend's, and I pictured the traffic thickening. I must have watched the house for longer than I thought. My best hope was that Zoe Porter would go out again. Somewhere below, with a muffled burbling, the kettle came to the boil.

I heard a key turn in a different lock, then a bolt noisily jolted. Zoe Porter was opening the back door. Go out into the garden, Zoe Porter, I thought. Go now, and I will leave and never come again.

The spare room overlooked the courtyard. I crept to the

window, parted the slats of Zoe Porter's venetian blind. I thought of everything in that house as Zoe Porter's. It's possible I thought her name so often to remind myself that it was her house. I looked down on the garden. Outside the kitchen, Zoe Porter sat on a bench – exactly where our bench used to be – with a mug on her knee. She looked peaceful. The sun was low, and made the wispy edges of her brown hair blond. She was slim. Her legs were bare and smooth. I was thinking that she looked about fifteen years younger than me when Zoe Porter turned her head to my window.

Did I just miss something? Kurt has stormed out of the room. Was he speaking to me? At the drawing room door, he drops Wendy into his belt bag, raises his middle finger and departs. I suppose it is progress. Using symbols is one of the oldest forms of human communication. But I can't stop now. I'm in the middle of this.

Zoe Porter and I reached the hall at the same time. To Zoe Porter's credit, she did not flinch. She looked at me, cool and firm. I think she must have seen that of the two of us, I was the more scared. I wasn't scared of her. I was scared of Kurt and what he would say and how I would have to stop going to the old house. I saw myself falling, falling, a tiny silhouetted figure dropping through the cracks in my marriage, in my relationship with my sons, through the turning circle at the dead end of the toilet-pan close.

She said, 'Did he send you?'

I must have looked confused.

'Because my cab's here in thirty.' She gestured to the case at the end of the wayfarer's bench. 'Better get on with it.' She had a look of authority, or disdain.

'Er, No, I'm Susan,' I said. Even as I said it, I thought how typical that I should preface my name with a negative. I heard my voice crack, making the Susan sound even worse than it usually does. Introducing myself has always been painful, but I was surprised by how deeply satisfying it felt to have landed my bad name in such a bad situation. Of course, there are two of us in the library (I am Susan B), but I avoid my deputy, lest co-workers start calling us The Two Sues again.

When Zoe Porter said nothing, I added: 'I wrote to you. This used to be my house.' At first Zoe Porter's expression did not alter. Then to my dismay she started to laugh.

My fingers had already gone to my bundle of keys and I was anxiously working free the ones to Zoe Porter's house. I held them out to her, and started to explain.

'Are they mine?' she said, intercepting them. She had stopped laughing. 'So you let yourself in and . . .' She looked behind her, down the hall, up the stairs, and I could see her panic. She was imagining me at liberty in her house.

Oh, it was awful! I stood and watched all this pass across her face. 'I'm very sorry,' I said. 'I thought my case was here. The one I wrote to you about,' I added, because her face showed no recognition. 'Desperate. My marriage is failing.'

Even as I said it, these words that I'm putting on the page were in my head, ghosting the words I spoke. I suspect this instinct is common in those who write, because an eminent memoirist visited the library last month for an event – Pauline and I had set out drinks and nibbles and turned the foyer into a sort of salon – and after I introduced the memoirist to our customers, she gave a short talk in which she described having this very instinct as she leaned over the corpse of her husband. (He had died in the garden while hanging out the washing.) She knew that her situation, appalling as it was, had to be written. She compared it to an out-of-body experience, because in that moment she understood that her writing self would bear witness to her physical self, and was already putting the horror into words. There was a gasp in the audience – because, after all, the husband was face down in the laundry basket – at which the memoirist looked up and smiled. She often told that story at events, she said, and there were always some who found her approach cruel, but true emotional acuity requires a degree of stone-cold detachment, which presents itself even, and especially, at moments of extreme pain. I don't know what more I said to Zoe Porter, but I know there was too much of it.

The words that fell out then will not fall out now. These days, I keep them closer.

It was the first time, as I stood there, that I'd said aloud to another human what I was up to. An expression of weary pity paled Zoe Porter's face, but I believe she was in that moment tougher than me. More 'resilient', in modern parlance. I intend to ask Susan to assemble a resilience selection for the new display table in the foyer. After all, who knows how long this 'austerity' era will last?

No explanation could justify my appalling behaviour, Zoe Porter said. Something along those lines. And she was right. As the policewoman observed when she took my statement later, I had broken into the house. I admitted it, of course.

'I'm so sorry,' I told Zoe Porter.

'What have you taken?'

I shook my head. 'If I'd found my case, I would have taken it.' I would.

Zoe Porter sighed. She did not seem hugely excited to have caught me. On the other hand, she did not seem ready to let me go. 'Maureen said she'd seen you.' She felt in her dress pocket and pulled out a phone. She was pretty, Zoe Porter, with her face cast down at her screen while she slid and tapped with varnished tips, her eyelashes long and dark against coffee-coloured lids. I downwardly revised my estimate of her age. What had become of me, to be standing in her hall in an un-spruce mac with my roots growing out while she decided what to do with me. I believe Zoe Porter knew I was harmless, but she was torn.

Well, I shall not relive every detail here. The door to my office is open and I would hate a co-worker, or customer, to see my words over my shoulder. Suffice to say, the police arrived at the same time as Zoe Porter's taxi. The cab parked behind the patrol car. In an absurd gesture of atonement, I paid the waiting fare while Zoe Porter explained to the police what had happened, and further explained that although this was her house, she was changing address for an uncertain period of time. I stepped away while she gave her details. The cab driver killed his engine. Maureen appeared beside the patrol car. Samirah came out of her house in a dressing gown and shower shoes. She shuffled down the pavement and gave me a hug, and chatted with me as if the police weren't there, as if no voices crackled in their radios, and offered me a drag on her cigarette. But of course, Samirah understood. The things I had in my heart to say, she didn't need to hear.

I felt so guilty. A bus passed, but only one passenger looked at me, despite the blue lights; I expect the others were busy on their phones. I tried to figure out what my mother would be doing, the time where Jilly was. I pictured Tam shaking her head and laughing at me, and I imagined Augustus in my reading room, and I found some relief in that. But Zoe Porter – I will not hear a word against her, for she saw that I was utterly lost, and later she withdrew charges.

I was awarded a caution, and it has not troubled me, and I think has evaded Cousin Richard's attention. The parents of the boys' friends gave them lifts. Just Kurt, who I had to call from the police station and who waited with the boys at home – and let us draw a veil over that conversation, because such shame and weariness I felt when I finally arrived back in The Close, and nobody took the blindest bit of notice of me. Neither son, nor Kurt, clustered at the island with their heads huddled over an amusing meme. I have not till now told a soul. But I saw Kurt's face. He lifted it briefly when I entered the kitchen, but he kept the lids shuttered. He continued to talk to the boys, and not me, about the opening of The Old Gables the following week, as if he were safeguarding them, or me. It was very upsetting. I did not need to be protected from the shame of what I had done. The shame of being detained on the pavement at forty-nine while a policewoman phonetically alphabetised my name into her radio was nothing to what I felt as Susan in my own kitchen. Sierra Uniform Sierra Alpha November sounded less pitiful to me.

In some measure, I believe Kurt must have been processing his own guilt, and although I did not enjoy the experience, I am glad of my crime and I am glad I was caught because without this catastrophe he would have kept me shut inside my little box of unknowing. But, see, he will not keep me, cannot keep me. When I'm busy like this, I feel free. Back then, everything seemed to be happening elsewhere, and now I am elsewhere, and Kurt knows it. And so is he, and that's how this whole thing started.

I suppose Kurt did not want to draw the boys' attention to me. But I wanted them to look at me, to talk to me, to lift their heads and throw me a word. And I wanted to ask why my eldest had paint all over his hoodie again. Instead I walked out of the kitchen with a glass of red wine wobbling in my hand, rubbing the spilled drops into the sisal with the sole of my sneaker, and it was with that feeling of being nowhere special that I came in here, to the desk in the drawing room, the room that none of us understood. I shut the interconnecting doors and I sat quietly until late in the evening – I was not then busy with this – when my youngest poked his head between those doors before he went to bed, and brought me a cup of tea, and he put his hand on my shoulder, and I lowered my cheek to his hand, and he told me it would all be OK, and I stood up and we met each other eye to eye, for he was the same height as me then, and we hugged.

It will all be OK.

I message Kurt. I share with him the photograph I took a fortnight ago of his precious tub of tech at the dump, with the skips in the background and this caption: 'If you want to see this lot again, you have twenty-four hours to return my case.'

Antony liked stones. He could pick one on the beach and tell you its life story. But theatre was his passion. He had other friends at Oxford besides me, also thespians. When he visited, we would see a play – the geology was becoming incidental – and eat at the Lebanese place with candles in straw-wrapped bottles. It was cheap but it did a good job of looking like a proper restaurant. Antony had a monthly allowance from his parents, so he paid for the two of us, and the friends, Michael and Sean, each paid for themselves, and we would talk about whatever play we'd seen. On the subject of which: I finished reading *Twelfth Night* this morning, and I cannot say I share the view of Malvolio as Hamlet-esque. He is a deluded grouch. I suppose it would take a performance to appreciate the complexity that makes 'the stars love to play him', as I have read in an internet article. I do not recall seeing *Twelfth Night* with Antony and his friends. Years later I saw in the alumni newsletter that Michael and Sean had married. Michael was the one with the nice face. Sean was the one who asked Antony questions all night and pretended he hadn't seen me. How's Liv? How's Tish? Did Kate get Cordelia? Always when I was with Antony, there was a string of names. Antony never elaborated. He never talked about the women those names belonged to. Chains of two-dimensional girls unravelled like paper dolls.

Well, it wasn't Liv or Tish or Kate or Tiggy or Hen. It was Silvie who, the next morning, Antony told me he was seeing. We'd spent the night – getting off with each other. As I say, I'm unsure that expression is still in use, and I dare not ask the boys, or Mika. Antony and I never articulated the terms of our relationship: we were friends, and we were lovers, and he was the world to me. But what this amounted to was not my place to say. His announcement came as a surprise. Silvie was brilliant. I was brilliant. I think he told me I would love her, or she would love me. The two of us would get on brilliantly. I was reeling but I didn't show it. I was eighteen, and I reasoned that I was still growing into myself. I was not yet the full me; it made sense that I was not enough for Antony, who was already very much the full him.

After Antony told me about Silvie, I walked with him over Magdalen Bridge – a couple in a punt passed beneath us – to the bus station. We shared a subdued farewell. I didn't want to mention Silvie or clarify where the news left me because I assumed this was our last goodbye and I didn't want to spoil it. That was the thing about Antony. Time with him was so precious, I didn't want to make a bad goodbye and lose a better memory. He embraced me tightly, raining the top of my head with kisses while I bit the inside of my cheek and widened my eyes so as not to blink. I watched him climb onto the coach with his rucksack on his back, just a small daypack that time, then I left. I hesitated to claim a greater role in his life than I now had. I could be the friend who walked with him, but I was so humble, maybe the money thing, it seemed a stretch to be the woman who waved him off.

I expected to hear no more from Antony. I imagined the moment when we would run into each other in Kent in the holidays; at the cinema or on the pier or beach – his parents' hut was not a million miles from my mum's flat. And maybe I would run into Silvie too. I spent hours rehearsing how our encounter might unfold. I would need to pretend not to want him if I were to retain dignity – something I worry even now that I know how to do only by denying a longing.

I moped about college, stayed in bed instead of going to lectures, avoided the bar. I kept a sheet of paper taped to the exterior of my door, where visitors wrote their names. Think of it as paper voicemail. Several times a day I heard friends come knocking, then scratch away out there with a pencil. When their footsteps faded down the stairs, and the door at the bottom of the stairwell slammed, I'd poke my head out and read the note. After a couple of weeks, some kind soul pushed my post under the door. The noise made me turn from my desk as a violet envelope, pleasingly fat, edged through the gap. I didn't need to see the handwriting to know who it was from.

After that, I emerged from hiding.

The letters came more thickly. I knew from occasional allusions to her that Antony was still seeing Silvie, but his letters were so fervent that this seemed irrelevant. Honestly, there was no less love in them than in the letters he sent before he got with her. Eventually I grew used to the idea that he had another woman. I suppose I should say he had a woman, since technically I was the other woman, being the one who lived elsewhere. I don't know. Neither expression is satisfying.

After a few months, Antony wrote to say that he and Silvie were no longer together. He was seeing Cheryl, who worked in a bar, and it was a relief to go out with someone who was not a student. He never told me we were not together, by the way. After Cheryl there was Sandy. After Sandy there was Mandy. I remember one of us made a quip about Antony's rhyming scheme. After Mandy I stopped keeping track. I knew that every so often there was someone new. The endings were barely remarked upon, which made me curious to know if those girls really had gone, or if Antony kept them up, as he kept up me. Maybe they passed like lost things, through friendship to occasional meetings then chance sightings till they were truly gone. Sometimes I wonder when I passed, which is silly, because whenever it was, it must have been a very long time ago.

Antony kept me in a state of uncertainty. The letters told me he loved me but did nothing to disturb the uncertainty. It seemed to exist independently of them, and they, the letters, had a confidence that was independent of us. On paper, we knew where we were. On paper, I knew he loved me. I guess Antony was a sort of paper man, and ours a paper love. It is good to get him on paper again like this, to have him to hand. If I can get him on paper, I can keep him on paper.

I am sitting in the kitchen, waiting for Kurt. Earlier today, I returned from the library and found my old case on the table.

My tan leather case. The very same. But not quite the same. The locks have pulled free of the leather. They dangle from the lid so that anybody could open it, and no doubt somebody has. It looks older than I remembered; smaller. I tap one of the locks and it swings. I do not feel as affronted by this as I would have done in Phase One, back when I ransacked all those boxes. It is not exactly the case itself that worries me now. My finger frets at the long gouge and my initials on the lid. Not mine, I mean.

I have been sitting with it for, let's see, nearly an hour.

What a shock to walk in here and – I can't even say I found it. More like it found me. On the table, at my usual place, with a brazenly matter-of-fact air.

My eyes dart around the room. They crave words, want to read every word they see: the label on the jar of peanut butter that the boys have left on the table, the story of the person who founded the muesli company, the business card from the removal firm, the letter from the boys' school about my eldest's attendance, the days of the week on the calendar, the numbers, copyright information, photographers' credits, the maker's name on my apron, hung on the peg.

I just need a minute while I picture, for the last time freely, the reams of lilac paper and streams of green ink. I cradle the case in my arms, rest my cheek on it, and my upper body begins to rock. I croon. Somewhere between singing and moaning, I inhale a waft of lavender, which may be because I have pictured lavender paper. The scent is very strong. I inhale again. It is Maeve's lavender. Well of course it is. Didn't I know it? Didn't I? More than with Kurt, with whom I have tuned my anger to a relenting detachment, I am angry at myself, because I have always been a hard worker, a diligent student, and every library feels like a home from home for me, even the ones in the schools and sixth forms I've been touring with the boys; yet I have reached the age of fifty, a number not massive but still quite large, without learning to trust my instincts, and to act on them. That has to change now, right now.

The boys enter the room. They have stopped saying hello, owing to their age, or the age we live in. 'Hello' is for old people. I'm not sure, but I think 'hi' might be too. The boys take juice. They take spreads. Leave crumbs. These days, the fridge is my main tool of communication. I am like Boo Radley in this house: instead of putting messages in a hole in a tree, I leave them on the middle shelf of the American-style fridge freezer. Neither son speaks. I clear my throat, a nervous habit I have developed since the incident with the police, and I say, 'Do you remember how I lost something when we moved here?'

Two blank looks.

'You were only twelve.'

Two disbelieving looks: they were never only twelve.

'Well, here it is,' I say, rubbing the lid of the case. My eldest glances at me, then back to the fridge. I tell him, 'It was here on the table when I walked in.' I watch him spread Marmite on a slice of bread, fold it twice and take a bite. I say, 'Was it here when you got home? Have you seen your dad?' He shakes his head, returns his earbud to his ear. My youngest has reached the door first, but hearing his brother experience the pain of enforced conversation moves him to look up from his phone. He keeps his thumb on it and says, 'And how was *your* day, Mum?'

———

Perspective requires that things far away be portrayed small, and I want to keep Antony in perspective, and contained, and tiny, and maybe that is why I have sat for a further half-hour in the kitchen with the lid shut. The Antony locked in here may be different to the Antony who lives in my heart, or in that place where love stores its waste. I have the sort of memory muscle that can pump a thing up big.

I'm not surprised to learn that the average person touches their phone 1,537 times a day, because this past hour I have picked mine up every few seconds. I keep unlocking it, then forgetting what I've gone in there to look for. I want to share my news with someone. But the only people who would understand are Mum and Tam, and I cannot tell them, because I have always been the sensible one and it is late to start now. I whizz down and up my frequently contacted. It is wrong to think of Mika. Cousin Richard rings out. On my way to the Forum, I change my mind and double back. All the numbers I have for Antony are dead.

Ten minutes ago, I tapped Kurt's name, but the call went to voicemail and the beep caught me off guard. I said ... I don't even know what. 'Did you put it there? You did put it there. Because it wasn't here this morning and it wasn't in the loft.' I rattled on and on. I blurted something about the smell of lavender under his mother's bed. I heard myself say, 'Why don't you speak to me? Why don't you answer?' The gaps between my questions grew. 'Why aren't you there? Why are you never here?'

Oh, what an enormous sigh! My free hand went to cup my free ear. And then a woman's voice cut in. *Sorry, your recording time has expired.*

Being true to my word is important to me, so I fetched Kurt's old tech from my burgundy trunk and deposited it on his workbench in the garage. Back in the kitchen, I ran the tap and listened to the water clatter into the metal sink, the only member of the family not to use the chill button. I held my fingers in the stream in a daze. And while I stood there – one of those small moments of everyday domestic entrancement – I realised for the first time that death was not something that was going to happen to me.

I am going to die, I thought, and it will be the last thing I do.

I am aware that the line between the momentous and the banal can be very fine, but bear with me. I thought, I will be me while I die. And whatever shift inside I feel, whether there is pain, or liquid, whatever shapes or spots pass behind my eyelids, no matter how much of my life I forget, that will be me, doing my death. I filled my glass and sipped the cold water.

While sirens wailed through the ceiling from the boys' computer game, I opened the lid.

———

A faint leathery scent rose from inside.

I sank my hands into the case and rubbed the papers between my fingers and thumbs. There were a few from my dad while I was at university, tooled in a very shaky thread. Several of Tam's ironic postcards from Leicester. I think there is also a letter in here from Jilly when she moved to Michigan. Nothing from Mum, obviously. She mainly kept a pen to fill in coupons.

Oh, but all I really saw was Antony. His hand was so distinctive that even when he wrote my name, his signature was all over it, on dozens of envelopes, bundle after bundle of his lavish ink and ravishing flourishes. I was rich with Antony. I had great wads of him. I thumbed the edges of the envelopes as if I were fanning banknotes.

The first envelope was postcard-sized. The paper inside had been trimmed with zigzag scissors. In tiny, unjoined letters in the centre of the card, it said, 'Friday. 4pm.' The next envelope contained the typed lyrics to 'Suzanne' by Leonard Cohen. There was no covering note, but Antony had changed all the Suzannes to Susans. I can still hear his tender, earnest voice singing the first line: 'Susan takes you do-own to her place near the river . . .' Somewhere in here is Antony's list of 'Muses called Suzes', top of them the young woman who was pictured with Bob Dylan on the cover of an album we both loved and who, I think I'm right in saying, wrote her own book a few years ago. Well-known Susans are hard to come by. How Antony pulled that list together before the internet I do not know. He must have spent hours in the library. In fiction, Susans are sensible children or spited wives. The Queen's first corgi was called Susan. I try to smile at the irony, when I hear him speak to her, that this new Siri character Kurt adores – I found this out – is actually a woman called Susan.

I love that letter of Antony's. It always made me feel a little gladder to be me.

The next envelope enclosed a train ticket to Edinburgh; the ticket is still inside. The next promised a visit. The one after that was an apology for having failed to show up. I steeled myself. I expected to find a few of those. There was a 'Chad' with the slogan 'Wot no Susan?' Most of the letters were signed 'Your

Antony'. My Antony, who was never mine. Or maybe he was, and lots of other people had their own Antonys too. I gorged on letters. I kept telling myself that each would be the last, that I'd save some, put them away till tomorrow. But I couldn't stop. I was desperate to find the one that said something absolute and inarguable. Somewhere in here was the letter that said 'I love you', over and over, till the ink ran dry and Antony scratched out his love with his bare nib.

But who am I kidding? I was looking for something that never existed.

I found one lone shark's tooth – who knows where the others went – and I found the lucky stone with the hole. I have it here beside me.

Letter after letter I took from the case. I devoured Antony's writings. In the library, Gerald wears gloves to handle our few rare books, which we keep in a locked cabinet outside my office. Antony's letters were not like that. They did not resemble historical documents to me, and I grabbed at them as if they were freshly sent, drawing out one after another while the cherry in the garden vanished into dark and the words became harder and harder to fathom, and the ink spot in my head wetly glistened. Now that I have switched on a lamp, I can see that in places Antony's green ink is turning grey.

Well, what to say. The longest letter contained no note of affection at all. It was a densely and electronically typed treatise on the monogamous traits of swans. It ran to five sides. Did I know that when a swan found a mate, they were mates for ever? This was unusual, Antony wrote. I say 'Antony wrote', but I imagine he plundered the words from some natural history of swans he'd found in Ravens, our favourite second-hand bookshop in Kent, a jumble sale (Google it) or the library. I'm not sure I read this letter properly at the time. I expect I would have seen immediately that there was nothing in it for me – no promise of a visit, no statement of love. It's a shame, because it is fascinating.

At the kitchen table, I spread the pages flat. There was a pair of swans in Bonn, Germany, who had been together for twenty-three years. One summer, the male became ill. The wardens in the park where he lived noticed that his beak had faded to a dull yellow. His movements slowed; his head drooped. There came a day when he didn't take to the water. He slumped on the bank; his mate kept watch. All day the cob refused to lift his beak. Sometimes he appeared to try, but the weight of his long neck pulled it down. In the morning, the wardens found him dead on the bank, his mate beside him. Three weeks later, the pen – that is the name for a female swan – died of a broken heart. 'The pen is mightier,' Antony wrote.

I looked up. The Close was quiet, always quiet. Just the distant drone of the building works, brought to me on a northerly wind.

Antony wrote: 'You know that you and I were meant to be together and always will be meant to be together.' I first read that sentence at my undergraduate desk. It was so cold, I read in fingerless gloves with a hand slid through the handle of my mug, leaning over the tea, which is why the letter has stiffened into crackly ridges. We were meant to be together, we will be meant to be together . . . Antony's was a sort of everlasting promise, which in practice was an everlasting deferral. We would always be meant to be together – without ever actually being together. My throat swelled. The words blurred. The sadness of it, sitting at my kitchen table with these letters finally in my hands, and saying all kinds of things I had forgotten they would say. He loved me, but not enough. I loved him, but failed to communicate this. I couldn't own my name, so what chance my feelings? And I am not saying it is like this for everyone who goes short. Just speaking for myself: not having money made it harder in almost every situation to find the words, and the voice to say them with. Had I done so, Antony may have loved me more. We may have sufficed.

I got up and walked around the kitchen. My youngest came in and stopped at the table. He looked at the mound of letters and shook his head, bemused. He said he could only read handwritten writing in capitals. He switched on the kitchen light. He went to the fridge. He left. I exhaled loudly as the yoga teacher sometimes invites us to do. There was no one else's breath to disturb.

In the next letter I unfolded, Antony urged me to dump him. He drew the swan upside down; its feet waggled from the bottom of the page. They were dark green, webbed, and possibly waving. At the library, we have scant stock on swans. I know they have spatulate bills and are dabblers, because Antony and

I visited a swannery in Dorset on our one and only holiday, but I think Antony's swan could equally be in its death throes, or hunting for fish. Days later, he wrote to plead with me to stick with him. He drew a cartoon strip of two swans necking. They had gone too far and knotted.

Antony was an incredibly meaningful person. I mean that he wrote promise into the tiniest things. He kept me searching for his intentions in his letters even when, as happened one time, the envelope arrived completely empty. I wondered if Kurt had found that one and discarded it, because it is not here, and God knows I have gone through this case. I was looking for the letter that told me he loves me. I thought, If I can just read that one, I can stop all this. What I lost, I can take. I will put these away, shut the lid.

Halfway through the case, I found it.

———

It can be hard to attend to the same three words on a loop. One knows what's coming. The eye jumps ahead, and the words lose meaning. But this letter posed a different challenge. It comprised a single page. And it did say 'I love you'. It says that many times. But I must decipher the words through the thick black mesh that Antony scribbled all over them. He was careful to leave large enough gaps for me to read through, and somehow, somehow, I remembered only the words, allowed them to imprint themselves on my memory, while erasing entirely the scribbling-out, this jagged black screen which now, miserably, is all I really see.

The inaccuracy of my memory floors me. It is as if I committed a certain view to mind and forgot that I had seen it through a heavily latticed window.

Why did Antony write, then cross out, then still send the letter – the entire version history on a single piece of paper? I felt myself plunged back into my student room, the messy desk suggesting some kind of struggle, the little three-bar heater I must never touch, the case on the hearth, the steam of my breath, the awful uncertainty about whether he loved me.

Antony was clever. His handwriting toyed with the letters, and I swear each *I love you* gave off something different. There were inclining ones and uptight ones, and stragglers that ran so loose the love barely held together. The ys of his yous hung tantalisingly, each descender dangling a tiny grappling hook for me to cling to. I believe he knew, in his blood and in his ink, that I was permanently scrabbling for a hold. But he let himself off the hook, edged off the page, sealed the envelope behind him.

I have sat here at the kitchen table a very long time, staring at this one disappointing page. Antony wrote it before he acquired an electronic typewriter. (Imagine a supersized laptop with a separate lid, and a screen so tiny that it fits only five words.) But how little difference the advance in equipment made. With his own bare hand he changed his font, type size, emboldened and undermined. He processed words long before we learned

WordPerfect. He broke them up, diced and sliced, and with only those three at his disposal, he made love seem so variable.

Antony sloshed his love extravagantly while I kept mine close to my chest, penned and absolute. I never told him the things I should have told him. His extravagance didn't rub off on me. The only way I knew to respect the value of those words was by never using them.

It is possible that Antony defaced that letter because he wanted me to wonder whether he did love me or whether the crossings-out meant he had, in the process of writing, discovered that he did not, and I was to view his letter as a real-time correction. I suppose that's something we have lost with electronic writing; the ability to see how – and when – a person reworks their words, as we all do. Maybe he was in two minds, scared of laying himself bare. Or was he trying to provoke me, to force me to act? I could understand that. What I cannot understand is why none of these thoughts occurred to me at the time, when I regarded Antony as masterful in our relationship yet failed to see the impact on him of my own overpowering reticence. I read about a forthcoming book this week in our trade magazine – by a woman called Susan, no less – which the article said will make introversion understood, and even prized. I've ordered two copies for the library.

Well, one person's letters tell only half a story, and in truth they are likely to tell a much smaller fraction than that. I do not recall writing to Antony that I loved him. I find myself wondering – and it is a lot to wonder so late in the day – is it possible that he didn't know? I look up. I stand. My feet cannot find which way to walk. I need air. I slide back the glass wall and step onto the slabs. The garden is permanently shady, but if I crane my neck and look directly above my head, I can see the sky, still blue, the clouds scudding. I learned that word in a library book as a child. I think I hear the cry of gulls, miles overhead, and miles from the sea. It seems absurd that Antony may not have known that I was desperate to see him as soon as we said goodbye. That I would gladly have assented to any arrangement, any commitment. That while I said nothing my heart was ringing.

It has become increasingly clear to me that he did not know. That is why I have begun to think about writing to him one last time.

I have tried so hard to keep Antony in the box.

I believe he needed a lot of love. Many of his letters were conceived as a trial. He tested me. And letter after letter, month after month, over six or seven years together, more when you count our little postscript, and however many years apart – because reading these letters somehow makes all the time without Antony feel like time with Antony – I failed. Do not try to talk me out of this. I lacked the assurance to tell Antony how I felt. So he said too much (wanting me to say more) and I said too little (wanting more) and neither of us gave what the other needed. We lost our future life, back when we could save it, before it became a shadow whose years I still count. But what if it isn't too late?

Antony's written words and Antony's intentions seemed to call each other into such complicated question. This was apparent in the smallest details, even the way he would open brackets in a sentence, then allow the letter to run on and on without the brackets ever closing, as he does in several I have here. Somewhere in my case is the one he processed in the shape of a sight test. He centred it carefully:

WHYDON
TYOUL
OVE
ME
?

I had always thought that Antony left himself so many places to hide. But now it is painfully obvious that I was the one hiding.

The letter I really wanted to read was a letter I would never find. Poorly blotted, ink-spotted, written in words I cannot recall, it was the last I wrote to Antony. I posted it to him, so it isn't in the case. Eighteen years ago, the stone with the hole in rolled cold and hard out of his final reply. The note he sent with it I binned soon after reading. But the stone – the stone found a way around my anger and my pain simply by satisfying my need to hold something, and I think that's why I kept it, because it had won its place, in place of something else. It doesn't look like much: a small piece of grey flint. But I lift the hole to my eye and aim at the sky, and it is the closest I have come to what I am looking for.

I fear I have lived my adult life inside one of Antony's never-ending parentheses. It is only now dawning on me that I can be the one to close those brackets.

Last night, I sat at the kitchen table long after I had shut my little leather case. I rested my head on my arms and my arms on the lid, and I waited till gone midnight for Kurt to come home. I thought, No more hiding now. But shortly before one, I collapsed into bed in the spare room, with the holey stone wrapped in my palm. In the morning, before I lifted my eyelids, I heard the front door click. It is grimly amusing to think that with the case in my possession, I have finally unpacked.

Today I went into work, but struggled to focus. All day I imagined how my conversation with Kurt might go. When I got home, my youngest son was in, and the eldest is here now – I heard him run upstairs with his backpack jangling – but still no Kurt. I took a deep breath and I faced the cushion on the main stem of the L where Kurt usually sits. I nodded a perfunctory greeting. I left a space for him to speak. This is also how sleep-talking works, by the way. It is a little-known fact that people who sleep-talk usually respect the turn-taking of normal conversation. And that's how my awake-talk went too.

'Why did you take it?' I heard myself say to the long blue cushion on the main prong.

. . .

'So I'm the one in the wrong! You stole my case. You lied to me, wasted my time. Years I've spent looking. You stole so much. You took my hopes. But I've got them back!'

. . .

'It *is* stealing! Cousin Richard said it was.'

. . .

'Except we can't, can we. You don't see me. I'm sick of looking at your eyelids with their twitches and spots. God, those eyelids are ugly!'

(I am not proud of myself, but I want to be honest.)

. . .

'I *am* calm. Unlike you when you saw me in your mum's spare room and dragged me across her carpet. Ha! No wonder you came rushing in from the garden! I had you then. I had you, and you knew it.'

. . .

_____

Do you ever get caught up replying aloud to something no one has said? I turned at a movement in The Close, and saw that bloody Glossop woman from the better Beaufort looking at me, and at the weeds in our garden. She raised a hand, and I know

171

she was beckoning me, no doubt to talk about the antics of my eldest. I waved, then I lowered the blinds and gathered myself. I was not going to get drawn into a shouting match with Kurt in his absence. So I calmly said, 'I think we can agree that it's neither unstable nor irrational to persist with an apparently hopeless cause. It's called resilience, and I believe the modern world will recognise its value.'

God, I sounded really strong. And petty. It was actually painful to hear myself. After the Glossop woman, I didn't have the stomach for it. 'Who gives a shit about the case?' I cried. 'This is not about the case! This is about you and your failure even to look at me or speak to me.'

. . .

'Oh Kurt! It's too late for sorry.'

I have barely finished talking when I hear the click-click of the garage door. I rush to put the letters in the case, the case beneath the desk. As soon as Kurt appears in the doorway to the drawing room, I just say, 'You found it.'

There is nothing else to say. Besides, after the business with the cushion, I feel as if we have already spoken. He indicates with a wary nod that he did find it, and I surprise him. I just say, 'Thanks.' And I smile an upside-down smile, because I want him to know that I am OK with what he did, that in this precise moment primarily what I feel is not anger, because who cannot look at Kurt and see that this is happening to us both, and it is very, very sad. I would like to touch him, to share this with him, but he is rooted in the doorway, holding the tub of

172

junky old tech that I left for him in the garage. I take a couple of steps, and I stretch out a hand and brush his wrist with my fingertips. It is all I can reach. Kurt glances at the place I have touched, turning his wrist inward as if he's checking the time, and he looks at me, and his mouth drops into the same unsmile that I gave him.

I feel calm. And I think this is partly because Kurt looks so awful. I cannot think when he last went to bed at a sensible time. His lids are yanked aloft on a dazed stare. It seems significant that he stands on the bald patch in the sisal. With both hands he clutches that tub protectively at his hip, his knuckles tight and yellow. He looks absorbed, absent, I mean, but in a different way to normal, because his absence is all over his face like an emotion, and I see that actually today he is here and he is deep inside himself, a long way in. He leaves the house through the front door and I turn back to my desk. My desk. My chair. My lamp. One day soon, I will have to put stickers on all of those.

And then I realise that Kurt was here and I didn't see Wendy.

Caught in my palms in its black leather case. Detached from the plug and detained. Not in any of the positions Kurt logged in his fieldwork. 'Thief'? 'Captor'? I am going to sit on Kurt's stool, have a little play and see what all the fuss is about. This is the closest I have been to one of Kurt's phones since old Wendy drowned in the washing machine nearly two months ago. I butterfly my hands to take a closer look, and it's funny, but holding Wendy, knowing that Kurt is without Wendy, makes Kurt seem even further away. I cannot help feeling stung, on his behalf, by how oblivious Wendy is to his pain. From the porthole window, I spy the traffic warden on the other side of the road. I place my finger on Wendy in the way I have seen Kurt do, to make Wendy open. Four empty boxes spring up. I type the year of Kurt's birth, 1959; our old and new house numbers; 1119, the time at which my eldest was born, 1120 (my youngest), 1920 for both. I am tinkering like this when the phone emits a high-pitched screech and shakes with a violence that makes my hands tremble. On the screen, the words *DEVICE ERASURE* begin to flash.

I shove the phone under my jumper. I take it out and sit on it. I press every 'button' I can find. I cannot shut it up, I cannot shut it down. The camera is going berserk. When I hear Kurt's key in the front door, I stuff Wendy under my armpit.

There is no time for instructional videos or the Forum. I lurch at the crate of tools and grab the sledgehammer. I crouch on the concrete floor and wait till the last minute to remove Wendy from my armpit and put it in front of me. It vibrates so wildly, it scuttles across the concrete like a startled animal. I still it with my foot. I wipe my palms on my thighs, and take a breath, a really deep one that I try to appreciate as it moves from my belly through my ribcage to my chest. Kurt didn't even apologise! I could have tried to understand, but he has no wish for understanding. He had nothing to say to me. He has a pair of foggy phone goggles for eyes. We have sold each other cheap for this piece of scrap. I raise the sledgehammer above my head. The lumpen weight wobbles unsteadily at the end of its long handle, as if to heave me backwards. I take one last look at Wendy's famously indestructible screen, then I shut my eyes and swing. The hammer handle leaps in my hand. There is a crunch, a squeak and a long, shrill whistle. My palm buzzes. One blow is all.

When I open my eyes, a thick black gap cleaves the glass of Kurt's Wendy, darker than dark and keyhole shaped. It is the centre of a new constellation: beautiful and brutal, the pattern of its shattering. I pick it up and grains of glass stick to my thumb. The warning message pixelates but the screen stays aglow. A strange sticky substance has seeped into or from the leather case. I won't be touching that. The kitchen door releases. Then the light behind the screen dies, and Kurt steps into the garage.

I get to my feet, back away. I kick a fragment of phone casing towards the carcass, so the pieces are all in one place. Kurt gasps as he passes me. I retreat till the cool metal door handle meets my hand. I reverse into the kitchen and quietly, very quietly, I close the garage door and lock it. All the levers run home.

Phase Three

Phase Three

A few things have happened. As you can see, I have logged off. I have picked up my pen. That is how we used to write, Antony and I.

'Ink is the heart's blood. Mine is green and yours is black,' you told me. 'Writing is like letting blood. So strap one hand around your wrist, squeeze up the veins, and write.' We wrote like that, hand over fist. I know it sounds teenage, but that was the point.

An hour ago, I drove to the old place with my best pen. No need to panic: I parked on the parade, well away from Zoe Porter's house. Then I dropped into the post office, where I bought myself this smart new exercise book, like we had at school, with a fibrous pink cover printed with 'Name' and 'Subject' fields, which I have left blank. I also bought an envelope and three sheets of Conqueror. Triumphant, I headed to the Continental. I plan to keep the letter brief: the three sheets are so I can start again if I need to. I expect I shall need to.

It has been a long time since I've put pen to paper in this way, Antony.

Listen to me! I am already writing to him and I have not yet found a seat.

———

Here comes the waiter with my coffee. Having called the theatre in Gateshead where Antony is about to start his run in *Twelfth Night*. I feel quite happy about this, believing that a small theatre whose mission is 'to spread a passion for the arts to our community' will take good care of correspondence.

> Dear Antony,
> It is so much harder than I remembered. I brought my best pen, but my nib is out of practice and squeaks over the paper. The only free chair is at the communal table. The man next to me has a tattoo in the shape of a Nike tick. I wonder if you can get one for Marks & Spencer.

I don't even cross it out. I just start below on the same sheet.

> Dear Antony,

The 'A' is ugly, so I start again.

Dear Antony,

Am I a surprise? You came into my head. A small internal knocking, and there you were.

Way too intimate. I tear the wrong words from the page. Although the tearing makes a lot of noise, the man next to me, the one with the Nike tattoo, regards his laptop intently. Hey, I'm the lady in the café, make that coffee shop, with a fountain pen, which I realise must be an anachronism to Nike guy and the woman on my other side, whose cables I worry are a trip hazard for the waiter. I push aside my coffee cup. Sunshine pours through the windows.

The funny thing is, when I talk to Antony, I don't see my words winging their way to him. He feels much nearer than that. I talk to the Antony in my head, and I admit, this experience is not hugely unlike talking to myself.

Dear Antony,

I guess this letter will come as a surprise. I doubt you have been thinking of me as I have of you. For some reason, you've been on my mind. How are you? How is Twelfth Night going? Well, I hope. I'm well. Did you know I had two sons? They are fifteen. I'm fifty! I guess you are too. Remember how old that was. I am still married, just. Married – Just. People should make a sign with those words and hang it on the back of the car as they head to the divorce lawyer.

Although I like the casual tone with which the letter starts, my voice becomes way too mawkish.

Antony, I'm worried. Are you OK? Antony, I'm worried. Am I OK? It's all right. I'm not asking for anything. Do you remember what you used to say about turning fifty? I bet neither of us thought I would be the one to come and find you. We thought we would be old then, but writing to you makes life move slower than time. I hope I shall be all right. Well, Antony, it's been nice talking.

It is too much. I fold the letter in half and stuff it into my bag with the other wrong letters. On the third sheet I write something like:

Dear Antony,
Hello. Well this is a surprise. It's been a long time. I'm in Gateshead next Thursday. I've got tickets for your show. Drink after?

Antony, are you there?

At King's Cross station earlier this morning, I waited on the concourse for my platform to be announced. I'm sure the renovations will look wonderful in time, but what a racket. I thought of the boys when I saw the little sign for Platform 9¾, quite hidden away. I took a photo to show them when I'm back. Given the popularity of Harry Potter, I'm surprised the station doesn't make more of it. As I scanned the destination boards, some old dread rippled my stomach. But here I am, with the fields speeding past the window, my wheelie bag stowed overhead, and in a couple of hours I will alight in Newcastle. It's a pleasure to feel the pen in my hand. No lifting of lids. Nothing to charge. I am at a loss to understand why more people don't communicate like this. I need only open my notebook and Antony is here, the ink syrupy with the closeness of him. It's as if we were all dried out and now . . . the page gleams wet and vivid.

Sometimes I unjoin my letters and space them out, and imagine I am dripping them onto you. Feeding you my words.

You, and not you.

I must be careful about that. Because since I picked up my pen, I have had to fight the feeling that I am writing to Antony, that that is who you are.

As I have said before, you are not Antony. And anyway, when I think of Antony – when I think of him – it is not Antony on a stage in Gateshead I see, nurturing an unrequited love for Olivia night after night. (I try not to dwell on that.) It's the Antony in my head, just out the corner of my eye, beyond the little doorway somewhere left of me, who slips through the hole in the stone or hides behind the deep, dark, frilling ink spot in my mind.

———

Now, where did I get to? Ah, yes. I was sealing my envelope in the coffee shop last week. It was hot, unlike today, where thick grey clouds roll past my speeding window. The waiter hooked back the door. People waited by the outside tables for someone to leave. I love how September sometimes belongs to summer, sometimes to autumn. The music played thin and tinny. I beat the café's lunchtime Wi-Fi curfew and ordered tickets for *Twelfth Night*. And yes, I suppose I did want to share my experience. I walked out of there tapping the envelope on my lip, in the manner of a person deliberating, and dropped it in the postbox.

And here goes Darlington. The train slows but does not

stop. On the platform, a woman struggles to retract the handle of her wheelie case. Then the station is behind us and we pick up speed.

All week I have lived in a strange elsewhere. After the boys released Kurt from the garage a fortnight ago – do not worry, he was only in there an hour or two – life outwardly continued as normal. I got up, the boys left the house, Kurt absented himself, timing his appearances so we discoincided. We seem to be separating very separately. I'm afraid I was extremely angry when I locked him in there. I can see how angry from the photographs Kurt emailed the next day, which show my face – I must say, surprisingly menacing – caught by Wendy's camera in the moments before Wendy's demise. I did not share those pictures in the Forum. After I told them what happened, Coryphe replied, 'WHAAAAAAT?' and someone else said, 'She gone too far.' Which was fine by me. I had left them behind. I paid for a replacement, incidentally. Even though a new model is forthcoming, Kurt refused to wait a few weeks. Apparently this particular one was special because it was launched by Steve Jobs, and Kurt feared it would be his last. And indeed, I gather he did pass away yesterday. According to the boys, Kurt will add the one I bought to his 'archive', as he calls it, and buy the new model when it's released next week. And that's OK, because I have finally figured out how to defeat a monster that always grows a new life. You walk away. You see, I helped to make Wendy. I gave the name. It is my monster too. So this is me, killing it off. It's just a phone. Kurt's phone. And it is Kurt's problem now. I wish I could describe my state of mind, but my head is all loose leaves blown to the wind.

Did I fantasise about Antony? I did. Sometimes I caught myself thinking that all I wanted was to share one last drink with him. Other times, I wanted to walk with him. Nowhere special. Beside the river or down the street, over Magdalen Bridge or along our beach, it didn't matter. Just to go alongside each other that little bit further. When Antony and I were together, I always had that yearning, and maybe that is why the lack of plan did not unnerve me. That was how we were. It was always one more night, one more day, one more kiss, one more letter. Until it wasn't.

Last night, I distracted myself with practicalities. I shut myself in the bedroom and confronted my wardrobe. I tried on dresses, jackets, best clothes, old clothes and new clothes with the labels attached. Each time I looked in the mirror, I baulked at my reflection's lack of resemblance to me. Not any sort of me that Antony would recognise. I refuse to wear a statement necklace just because I am fifty.

While I packed, an exchange came to mind that I overheard decades ago, when I was in sixth form and worked Saturdays on reception in a care home. Being younger, I tended to hear conversations rather than join them. One day, I overheard the manager compliment a junior administrator on her outfit. I desperately wanted to turn to look. I was too timid! So I have no idea what she wore. But I do remember this young woman's reply, which she voiced with wonderful conviction. She said,

'Dress for the job you want.' Dress for the job you want! It is a brave way to live, because it requires a person to admit what they want, and then show others.

Newcastle is the next stop; that's where I alight.

I will only add that I have not dwelled on frivolous stuff. I have not painted my nails. I have not bought anything new to wear that I will not later return. I do not want you to think me silly or excitable. I will not behave like a protagonist in a coming-of-age story. Besides, they usually take place in summer, and up here it's definitely autumn. I do wonder if mine is a sort of coming-of-middle-age story. And please do not think that pitiable or self-centred, because it is a fine thing to catch yourself in the act of ageing, to let yourself be at once the younger and older person you feel you are, without flinching or disownment.

Well, I arrived in Newcastle a few hours ago. Beside the river, the wind, which last week blew me so warmly from the coffee shop to the postbox in South Hill, had an icy edge. There was a text from Kurt that said *Can we talk?* It was not a good time. I walked to my hotel. Room was fine. I unpacked. With several hours before curtain-up, I rehearsed the thirteen-minute walk from hotel to theatre. Wide steps led to a row of glass doors in heavy red frames. The doors were locked, but the foyer was lit. What a thrill to be going to the theatre again! It hit me then that Antony must be inside, that we were the closest we had been in years. The Antony in my head smiled.

The stage door was at the side of the building: it too was red, but with no glass to look through. How I would have liked to slip inside and sit at the back in the dark watching Antony rehearse, a private performance that even he would have been unaware of giving. But this felt fanciful. I came back to the hotel. And now I must get ready.

I have brought only one change of clothes, having decided

to dress as if Antony and I were meeting as people who meet often, too comfortable in our skins to worry about outfits: jeans, a sweater, the cheap gold shark's tooth pendant he gave me for my eighteenth birthday (I wear it occasionally, so this is not a loaded choice), shoes that could belong to someone younger. The performance starts in two hours. I should eat, but I don't feel like eating. I need to open a window. This room has no thermostat. I have looked everywhere. The heater is blowing out air I don't want. I should probably dial zero but I want to be alone. I'm going to wear the same amount of make-up as usual, but apply it with more care. I am running out of time.

Did you know that the word 'want' comes from the old Norse 'vant', meaning lack? I have been thinking about how Antony always left me wanting. Left me in a state of desire, and left me feeling that I was lacking. Desire comes from something missing, I have decided. A gone thing passes, a sought thing slips the eye, and in its space a strong want grows.

The summer after I graduated, Antony and I holidayed in Dorset. Well, it was his field trip, and I joined him. We stayed near Chesil Beach, which Antony said is where geologists go for a roll in the stones. A famous book was set there a few years ago, but we did not have the sort of problems those characters had. The trip completed Antony's penultimate year, and after that we practically lived in his parents' beach hut, unless he had friends visiting, in which case I took extra hours at the care home and left him to it. Long, sunny days we spent in Kent. I know there must have been rain, but I don't remember it landing. Not like the golf-ball drops that pelt my window. I do recall that his mother kept a very verdant garden. You could lie on their grass, luxuriant as deep-pile carpet, and hear the waves hit the shore. We were always outside. Walking, talking, swimming. I don't remember the words, just the feel of it. I never had much money, but we didn't need it. In those days, there weren't coffee shops on every corner. If we were thirsty, we shared a can of shandy, or ransacked the fridge in the beach hut. It was always stocked with orange juice and French cheeses wrapped in paper.

At low tide we liked to comb the foreshore for shark's teeth. You could find them if you looked for long enough. Anybody could. We slid down those steep shingle banks and we goggled those endless acres of pebbles, chips and flecks of flint stacked as far as the eye could see, with plenty of whelk shells and chalk, the sedimentary rock being so prominent in that part of east Kent. This was a seemingly impossible mission: what chance to find a sliver of fossilised tooth? The trick was to look and not look, to let your eye scan rather than search, to be open to something that broke the pattern – an anomaly, a disturbance to the randomness of the shingle, a scrap or shard whose shape met the eye unaccidentally. That's what I looked for. I was very patient back then. And even though Antony was the geologist, I was the one who found the teeth.

Oh well, who cares about bloody shark's teeth. They never won me any prizes. I am putting this away now. The carriage I'm in – did I say? I am on the train home – has become stuffy and noisy. It stinks of instant drinks and pungent crisps. A woman on the other side of the aisle is video-calling someone she's sleeping with tonight and doesn't give a damn who hears.

The attendant is chinking his overpriced tea trolley two rows behind. Oh, don't mind me! I'm just tuning my pain experience. I am tired. Deeply tired. I need time. I need space. I need none of these things. I'm going to close this now. I want to be properly, thoroughly alone, and sit here and look at my phone for a bit.

I left the hotel at five to seven and set off for the theatre.

What else to note? Like I said, I was wearing jeans. Nothing special.

When I left my room, I avoided looking in the mirror. In the elevator, I kept my eyes on the doors. I handed over my key to the concierge and ignored the mirror above the desk. I did not want my reflection to see me. That may help to explain why it has taken me more than three weeks to sit down to write this. Also, there has been much to organise.

I stood for a moment in the shelter of the hotel porch. A light drizzle hung in the air. I opened my umbrella and stepped outside. Since I was alerted to Antony's role in this production back in August, on a joyful Wednesday afternoon in the reading room, I'd pondered outfits and transport, read reviews of historical Malvolios and researched hotels. But now the performance was an hour away, I began to feel underprepared. I snorted a little smile and muttered some witticism to the Antony at my side. He knew what I meant.

The sound of my voice brought me back. I looked around. Luckily there was only one other pedestrian, too far ahead to notice. But a man in the passenger seat of a parked car smiled at me, and I hated to have been caught on my own with my lips moving, a lonely lady talking to herself – till I remembered that saying stuff aloud while walking alone is perfectly normal these days. It means you have friends. I raised my eyebrows to the man in the car and kept my pace.

I pictured Antony in a dressing room, pulling on a pair of yellow hose. Perhaps he had someone to help with that. In the years we were together, and not together, Antony was always the one on stage, and I was the one in the audience. I suppose this time is a little different.

In my final year at university, Antony posted me a train ticket. He met me at Edinburgh station and we walked up to the castle. I went only that once. I think I worried that he might act on his belief, often asserted, that I would get on with Silvie/Mandy/Sophia/Sandy. By then we were several years into our love affair, but it was unclear to me, even when he reached his arm around me as we left the station and kissed my cheek, whether he saw me as his guest or his lover. Anyway, I went up there with all my best stuff in my bag, and my bag I left in Antony's room; he shared a flat with another geologist, called Fozz. After a small amount of sightseeing, Antony left me to explore with Fozz while he went off to the theatre to prepare.

I arrived at the stage door an hour before curtain-up to wish him luck. A student in a black polo neck wordlessly pointed to his dressing room. I knocked and pushed open the door, and there was Antony kneeling on a large tasselled floor cushion. He was bare-chested. Behind him, a woman in full stage make-up, hair scraped into a straggly bun, was rubbing his back. She was also kneeling, and she too was bare-chested.

They both looked up. I tried to appear nonchalant about the woman's breasts, which were larger than mine. She continued to stroke Antony's shoulders, and Antony smiled a little frownish smile to indicate that his submission was work-related. 'Pre-performance massage,' he said. He held out his hand for mine, and pulled me down in front of him to kneel. The room was not dark, but a couple of tea lights flickered by the mirror, which struck me as quite New Agey for Antony (this was in the days before scented candles). The woman's head was tilted and she gazed intently at Antony's back. A tub of oil was open beside her, and the air was thick with patchouli and coconut. My presence did not appear to affect her concentration; she may have been studying his moles and freckles. When he introduced me, she gave a friendly enough smile, and kept rubbing his back. I could tell from the movement of her arms that she rubbed quite low.

'Are you OK?' I asked Antony. I felt it was incumbent on one of us to acknowledge the massage situation. There was the woman at his back, kneeling, and me kneeling in front of him. I brought my legs around to sit, so at least she and I were not symmetrical.

'Thanks, Anna,' Antony said. He pronounced it Ah-na.

She sloped her hands slowly off his shoulders, and exited,

knotting a shawl around her breasts. The door shut behind her. 'What's wrong with your back?' I asked Antony.

He rolled his shoulders. 'Cold,' he said. Cold! I think he told me that Ah-na was very good. She massaged him every evening, despite having her own performance to prepare. I tried not to look sullen. I wanted so much to touch him, but I worried it would undermine the effect of his massage. In half an hour, the play would start. So I touched my finger to my lip and put it on his. 'Good luck,' I said.

He laughed, delighted. He called me quaint. As in, 'You are so quaint!' He pulled me to him and his back was perfectly fine because he rolled me over and we made love with the little candles flickering over his slippery skin, coconut oil slicking under my fingernails. We were just finishing when someone knocked on the door and called out, 'Ten minutes!'

I reached the theatre in Gateshead nearly an hour before curtain-up. The stage door was propped ajar and a couple of people stood outside smoking. Not a polo neck in sight. In the foyer, steamy from the heating and the rain, I bought a programme and took it to the bar. I ordered a gin and tonic and drank it strong at a table with a view of the door. Did Antony still have pre-show rituals? I pictured a soft-breasted actor in her fifties massaging Antony, and the Antony in my head sniggered.

I draped my coat on my chair, and went to the bar for another drink; when I returned, a man was sitting at my table. Not Antony, daft! I made a fuss of straightening my coat so this man in a blouson leather jacket would understand it was my seat. I sat. I took out my phone and checked it, a silly nervous habit. There was a missed call. I didn't tap to see whose. Someone had left me a voicemail. I turned the screen face down. This is my compromise with myself: I have a phone, but I am not tethered to it.

I wanted to seem not alone – hence the bloody phone – but also really to be alone. I needn't have worried. Anyone looking at me would have assumed that I was in a relationship with the man opposite, because he too was on his phone. I started to think of Kurt, so I moved my phone into my bag and pushed it down beneath the hairbrush and peppermints. I opened the full-colour programme and flipped the pages, the logos of the poultry farmer, sportswear apparel outlet, and alternative therapist who had sponsored the show, the trustees' welcome, the precis of *Twelfth Night*. And then there was Antony. Antony over half a page. Antony in that ubiquitous black-and-white shot – he always did prefer black-and-white – with lustrously swept locks. Antony with the half-smile I knew so well. Seeming to say, 'Hello, madam, and what brings you here?'

Another man, a friend of the first, approached the table and took the last free chair. This made me look more obviously alone, but soon the bell rang and a recorded voice announced that the performance would start in ten minutes. Chairs clattered.

People grappled with their coats. I had taken a seat by a radiator, a childhood habit, and several people came to fetch umbrellas and wet coats. I slipped my programme – which, by the way, mistakenly describes Antony as forty-six – into my bag, and joined the throng at the door.

I knew my ticket by heart, but I felt grateful to the usher. I wanted all the help I could get. My seats were in the fifth row. The plural is correct. And yes, it was odd to have bought two. In my head, I may have allocated the second seat to Antony. Not thinking he would watch the play with me. I'm not that silly. I just felt he was with me. Throughout this enterprise, I have felt the presence of a person beside me. Do you ever have the sensation that someone else is there, someone who understands everything you need an other to understand? Because if you do, let's say the seat was for you. Some things you just have to accept. What doesn't make sense can still be true.

The usher shone her torch for me into the centre of row E, lighting a pair of empty red cushions.

————

The seats flipped back as people in my row stood to let me pass. I glanced at the stage, hidden behind swags of red velvet. I stowed my coat and bag beneath my seat. There was a text from Kurt. I read the notification but not the message, and switched off the phone.

People bobbed up and down in their seats, called from row to row, overpowering the classical music that the Palace Theatre had provided. The red seats were pretty hard. I became conscious of what my yoga teacher calls my sitting bones. The woman next to me opened a bag of wine gums. I used a fingernail to clean my fingernails. I fished in my bag for my peppermints. I checked my phone was off. I reminded myself that I did belong there. I belonged there more than any of them.

I stood to let a couple pass and when I sat down I had to get comfortable again. All the while I had this rising sensation that my life was about to end. That I had walked into some incredible scarlet obliteration chamber.

Well, we're here now, I said, or thought, or said to the Antony in my head. Lights dimmed. The classical music stopped mid phrase. Voices lowered, tailed off. I had the sense that something was moving, rising, from my heart to my throat to my mouth, a scream or a song. The man to my left turned to look disapprovingly at the empty seat between us. I shrugged and tutted to indicate that it had nothing to do with me. I didn't want anyone to think I'd been jilted. That spare seat began to feel like a bad omen to have inflicted on myself.

Oh Antony, I am pressing my nib hard and my face leans into my notebook in the drawing room in this boxed-up desolate house. We were so close. You were waiting in the wings. And I was waiting in the stalls.

The curtain slowly rose.

And there was someone – not Antony – in the centre of the

stage, an interior of a stately building, two men attending him. Quite a traditional rendition. I waited for Antony to make his entrance. Several scenes passed. Each new character to move or speak I scrutinised. I had taken it for granted that I would know Antony the second I saw him, but would I? He would not look like my Antony. He would not speak like my Antony, or move like my Antony. And, of course, if you know the play, he would not immediately be wearing those famous yellow stockings. I scanned the darkened heads of my fellow theatregoers. What were all these people doing here on a rainy Thursday night? A laugh swept up from the stalls behind me, and I turned again to the stage to see what was so funny, and there was the clown, and next to him, Antony.

There is something in a loved human that is always, irrefutably, them. Because nearly two decades had passed since I last saw Antony. He broke my heart, though I was grown. And there he was on stage, wringing his hands, and even as he pretended to be someone else, good as he was, I saw him, saw whatever spirit it is that propels a person's limbs, lifts and lets gravity work on them in a way that is recognisably theirs. It was not the curve of his calf or the dip of his shoulder or the shadows under his cheekbones. It was nothing you could run a pencil around. It was the force that animates all those things. He didn't need to move a muscle and I could see it. In this moment when he was supposed to be someone else, he was inescapably Antony.

I watched him: silent, waiting his turn. Antony, the jobbing actor who was listening for his cue while holding this rather strange gait of Malvolio, with his right hip exaggeratedly jutting and making odd, superior twists with his hands. But I saw his head bow, his chin lower, a small dip of understanding. I saw him flinch, a dejected continual wobble of the head. Was he dejected?

I had an excellent view of Antony from the fifth row, and now I began to fear that Antony might have an excellent view of me. I felt myself redden. I cursed the empty chair beside me, which seemed to glow scarlet each time a particular spotlight shone. I fretted that it would be glaringly obvious from the stage, that in this sea of obscure head shapes, an unoccupied space, something that broke the pattern, as anomalous as a shark's tooth in a shingle bed, would be exactly the thing to draw the eye.

Antony turned to face me.

His eyes fixed on me. His head did not wobble. Though it was dark, I smiled. I felt so proud of him. Was he looking at me? Or was I another inscrutable lump in a haze of indistinct outlines? Our eyes did lock. I don't know if he was acting that bit or not. And then he was speaking, and really it was cruel the way the other characters mocked him. Because he held himself throughout with immense dignity, even in those criss-crossed garters. Having watched the performance, I do not see why Malvolio gets such a raw deal. I know he is a trifle pompous, but goodness knows, there are worse crimes in Shakespeare. As far as I can see, his only offence is to love someone above his station who doesn't love him back, and to think highly enough of himself to do so. But he is too solicitous, I suppose, and that is itself a kind of presumption. Honestly, you can't win.

Antony has done really well, I thought. He finished his

geology degree, and although it wasn't the best result in the world, he could have forged a career in that field. Instead he kept faith with his artistic passion. He never bailed on acting, and all these years later, he still lives by it, his work including – I got this from the programme – a string of pantomime roles and outreach work in prisons. And here he was on the opening night of a packed theatre. I wondered if he earned enough to get by, or if he relied on his parents. I thought of the box house, with its spacious rooms. And Kurt, Kurt in person, at home, project-managing across multiple platforms without his wife's reflection scowling at his eyelids. The words of the play passed through my head like a vapour.

———

On stage, Antony held a letter that resembled my letter. The ivory paper was stiff, not unlike Conqueror, and the ink was dark. My hand went to my heart, and my heart seemed to grow in my hand. Oh, I am doing it again now! What urge is it that sends my hand to my heart, so that I sit here at my desk in the drawing room, my heart in my left, my pen in my right? The one pumps, and the ink flows.

The letter Antony held on stage was from the woman he loved. Except it wasn't really from her. It was from another character pretending to be her. The idea was to make him look stupid, and bully him. Antony, whose face was horribly

204

disfigured by a strange smile the play required him to wear, got a lot of laughs, but I'm not convinced he wanted them. The man to the left of my empty seat needed his hanky to contain his high-pitched whinny. But I refused to join in. It was cruel the way the audience mocked Antony's character. His cheeks looked dreadfully hollow. I tried to decipher what he might be trying to communicate to me, if that were indeed my letter. Did he mean that I was or wasn't, had or hadn't been his love? It was always hard to know, more so now. I wished I had booked row A, then all of this would have been clearer.

Well, you probably know the story of *Twelfth Night*. Suffice to say, Malvolio's love is not requited. When the curtain fell and rose and fell and rose, I heard the man to my left say that Malvolio was a bit uneven. 'I think he's meant to be!' I butted in. For what it's worth, I think Antony did an excellent job. I know that I felt uncomfortable at the way he was treated.

The lights came on and the applause ended. Seats thudded back. My neighbours hunched over, pulling belongings from between their feet. I slipped my arms into my coat. In this light, the place looked shabby: there were bare spots on the red velvet, and the floor was littered with plastic cups and sweet wrappers. This seemed disrespectful to me, and I stooped to pick up a few bits, including my neighbour's wine gum bag, then joined the line of folk edging along the row to the aisle, and up the stairs, and all of us a little dazed by the brightness, blinking into the foyer.

I had made no arrangement with Antony. I had written

simply . . . Well, I'm afraid that here I have to admit to a documentary shortfall. I do not know exactly what I wrote. This, alas, is one of the limitations of paper letters. I kept only the scraps with the words I didn't send. I know I told Antony I was coming to the show. I remember that I specified the day. But did I ask him for a drink, fix a time, a place?

The foyer was busy. Outside, the rain slanted hard; people jostled in the doorway. There was a flapping and popping of umbrellas unfurling. I heard more than one sodden cry as cars rolled to a halt in the puddles. In the din of rain and yellow lights, I considered what to do.

One option was to locate Antony's dressing room. I tried to picture him in there, but all I could summon was Ah-na in the theatre in Edinburgh, so I went to the bar and ordered another gin and tonic. Antony would need to remove his make-up, hang his costume, and much as I hated the thought, he would probably need help to unlace those garters. He would dress, share a few words with the cast, and hopefully he would not sneak out through the stage exit.

I chose a seat by the window: I could see the road, as well as the entrance to the bar. I sat there sipping my drink too quickly, wondering if I would be better off elsewhere. After quarter of an hour, two women entered to a kerfuffle from a group at the large round table in the centre of the room. I recognised 'Olivia' from her photograph in the programme. I rummaged in my bag to switch on my phone. I avoided the messages from Kurt. I checked my emails; among them an invitation to farewell drinks at the little library, to mark its final day of operation. I tracked a delivery. I felt acutely and visibly alone. If I don't check my phone, I get a funny feeling that I'm facing the wrong way. I'd left my notebook at the hotel, so I typed a few thoughts into email.

'Hello, you,' he said.

His voice was above, beside me. His words: I worry they will sound cheesy.

But that's not how they sounded to me. I liked hearing him call me 'you'. That's how I often thought of him too.

I stood. We hugged. I refused to do so shyly. I held him tight, his shoulder blades in my palms. My stomach found his stomach. I tried not to contemplate whether this was how it used to feel. Antony brought his hands to my shoulders and gently steered me back, saying, 'Well, let's at least have a look at you.' He exaggerated a sidestep, cocked his head and examined me in that pretending way, with one hand on his chin. I think he was also really looking at me. Eventually he said, 'You look great. I need a drink.'

I assumed we would walk to a pub, that the theatre would feel too much like work, and no offence, but it wasn't the loveliest space in the world. But Antony was already heading to the bar, and I followed him. We weaved between tables, skirting the large round one where Olivia was holding court, and here we got stuck, because people kept standing to tell Antony how fabulous he was. I had not yet had a chance to tell him this myself. No one appeared to register me. But I affected a knowing smile – I knew Antony better than any of them – and encouraged myself to be patient. I'd waited years. What difference a few more minutes?

We finally reached the bar. I saw, over Antony's shoulder, the barman nod. The shimmery reverse of his waistcoat strained as he bent into the chiller cabinet. People were jammed two deep and the bar stools had heavy legs and I could not reach Antony's side, I could only stand behind him. He wore loose cords – he may still worry about his slim thighs – and a tweed jacket, whose lining had come loose at the rear, and which might have been ironic. For a while when we were young, he dressed like David Bowie, eye make-up, waistcoat and combed-back hair. People pressed beside me, behind me. It would have been easy to lose Antony, so I stretched out my fingers and held the hem of his jacket. I held on quietly while the barman set a glass on the counter, tipped in tomato juice, drops from various bottles, a celery stick; I just stood there holding this rough bit of cloth, its unstitched satin lining slippery. Antony was almost a foot taller than me, and my nose levelled with the space between his shoulder blades. I breathed in.

When I think of Antony's distinctive smell, it is the magnificent bedroom in Kent I feel around me – at the back of the house, on the top floor, always warm, the warmth somehow deepening the scent of him, the saltiness of his pebble collection dotted along the sill, the musty, pleasant odour of unaired carpets, second-hand records, cardboard, keyboards, squash rackets and guitar strings, things that had not seen the light, bargains procured, to his mother's dismay, from local jumble sales. I wondered if this tweed jacket had come from such a place. It was only inches from my face. I was in my old place, at Antony's back, a kind of flashback.

———

It took me months to get over Antony when it ended. Because it didn't really end. After I graduated, we had an intense summer in the beach hut, and then the next year he graduated, and over the following two or three years our affair became very intermittent. The intermissions lengthened. Antony got a job at the British Geological Society. He was rarely in Kent, while I still lived with my mum and sisters and freelanced for a copywriting agency. Eventually they gave me a contract; but by then, Antony had moved on. There was no final word on our relationship: we just put distance between us, and neither one tried to persuade the other that this was something we should navigate. It wasn't that I stopped loving him. I just didn't see myself as decisive, or persuasive, or able to try. I looked for jobs. I went on dates. I found a flat share. I moved to a different copywriting agency. I applied myself to my work and my social life as if I were administering a cure.

Perhaps because things had never really ended, I did not feel surprised to run into Antony, quite literally, one midsummer day a decade later. It was 1993, and we were outside the British Museum. I had dropped into an exhibition after work, and

Antony was walking to his shift. It was a difficult time for him. He had finally given up his job at the British Geological Society, against his mother's pleadings, to concentrate on acting. To pay the bills he took seasonal work on the reception desk of a four-star hotel in Bloomsbury.

We did not discuss our personal lives. I mean, everything was intimate with Antony. He heckled me about my work, which felt sort of meaningless to me, and encouraged me to look for a job related to my passion for books. But neither of us mentioned whether we had partners, what we did when we were not at work. We were in our early thirties. I didn't want to know his situation, and I didn't understand mine. Kurt had only just asked me out on a date; we were due to meet at Canopy for that first dinner on the Friday.

The next week, Antony and I began to hang out after his shift. We settled into a routine. This was before either of us had mobile phones, so the routine was how we knew where and when to meet. I guess I could have gone home and dialled up, but I don't think I had Antony's email and I doubt he checked. We were very much in-person people. At around half five each evening, I would hasten down Gower Street towards Antony, or he would amble up to me and wait outside the office. If he was working a late shift, we didn't meet, but I would call into the hotel on my way home and enquire about the room rate. This was acting practice for him. Sometimes when I went to the hotel to play this trick, he was not there, and on those occasions I stayed in the revolving door and came back out.

The evenings we coincided, we would walk, sit in a park, drift around an exhibition, get a drink. His parents had become less generous since he spurned geology, so neither of us had much cash. But it was OK to sit outside a pub for hours with empty glasses, to sprawl on the grass of a public square. It cost nothing to go to a gallery. Later, we'd catch the Tube together. My stop came first. Usually we would disembark, go back to mine and make out; he always got the last train.

One night, after two or three weeks of this routine, I collected him from the hotel, and he told me he had booked a table for dinner. Antony was very sophisticated; his mother was half French (she was the person who introduced me to garlic bread). The bistro he chose resembled a living room. Each table was dressed with a white linen cloth. We arrived early and had the place to ourselves. Candles with elaborately melted wax were stuck fast to little ceramic dishes. The waiter wore a crisp black suit. We took our seats, and Antony announced that he intended to pay, and I should follow my heart's desire. I thought to choose chicken chasseur, but when the waiter came to take our order, Antony declared chicken chasseur too modest, and insisted the waiter bring me lobster thermidor.

It was the most wonderful meal, but even though Antony was paying, I was petrified by the cost of that lobster. I picked away at it – I did not know then, as Antony surely did, that thermidor is lobster for beginners. It was invented in France in the nineteenth century. All I thought was: This is finally happening. And, I will have to tell Kurt I can't make that second date. The white tablecloths, the formality of the waiter. Everything felt so official, celebratory. My awareness of my happiness hovered around the happiness itself like a heat haze. And around that, the worry that I did not deserve this joy.

The waiter cleared our plates, and Antony ordered dessert to share. Possibly in protest, the waiter brought one spoon. Antony and I took it in turns to squelch it into the crème brûlée. While the spoon passed back and forth, Antony held my free hand and told me that he loved me. I felt so happy, it embarrassed me; I felt that to see me so happy, he must have known how desperate I was to hear those words. His blue eyes glittered intently, moistly. He seemed to be asking for something, which was unlike him; support, understanding? I remember thinking, This moment will change us. I smiled, my hand hot in his hand and I squeezed his hand hard. I wanted him to know that I loved him too.

We had the whole evening at my flat ahead of us, but we were in no rush. After dessert, Antony ordered coffee. After coffee, petits fours. Neither of us wanted the meal to end. By the time we reached the Tube, it was long after ten.

Oh well, who gives a shit.

It has nothing to do with what happened in Gateshead. It was twenty years ago.

People were jostling to reach the bar, but Antony detained the barman and ordered me a – 'Gin and tonic,' I said. I had to raise my voice. I tried not to feel miffed that he needed to ask. 'Aren't you drinking?' I wanted to pay, but no money changed hands. Antony turned to face me, his eyes a murkier blue than I remembered. He lifted our drinks clear, while people thrust forward to fill our place at the bar, and we were pressed body to body. It was so hot. There was a smell of damp wool, wet coats drying on radiators, windows steaming. Someone turned up the music, and I experienced a kind of lightening behind my eyes. My thoughts broke in a mess of jumbled letters.

I felt myself go—

I could not arrange words, did not know words, had only a wordless sense of personal dispersal. Carpet bristles fuzzed my cheek. I tried to think what but my head was a tapping that went too slow. I was dully aware of the enormous effort my mind was making in that moment to reassemble myself. It was only when I heard Antony say, 'She's all right', and realised that

I again knew sense, that I understood I was OK. Something wet and unpleasant landed on my forehead. Icy drops rolled thickly down my skull beneath my hair. I thought it would be possible to open my eyes, but they were pinned shut. Then a hand soothed my cheek, warm and caring. I pictured Antony's. There was his voice, close, asking for space. Shoes shuffled. A chair leg scraped. The air around me thinned, cooled. The wet bar towel was removed from my forehead. 'I know you're in there,' Antony's voice said. I smiled. I opened one eye, then the other. I had the sense that I was stepping off the edge of something, nothing beneath my feet. Well, I was lying on my back.

Antony enlisted help to get me to his dressing room. I was raised to my feet. Someone applauded. They – Antony and another man – pretty much carried me, my toes skimming the ground, through a swing door, then another, down a passage and into a tiny room with the same red and gold carpet that swirled everywhere. A dressing table was pushed against one wall. Over the back of the only chair dangled Antony's yellow hose. They lowered me onto the seat. Antony fiddled with a window. There was a rhythmic dripping from the gutter, traffic on the main road. The air was good, the sounds rinsed clear. The man who had helped to carry me disappeared and returned a few minutes later with a tomato juice and a Coke. The Coke was for me. 'For the sugar,' he said. He wore thick black eyeliner. I think he may have been the Duke. I never did catch up with my gin. The Duke left the door ajar behind him and Antony pushed it shut.

'I'm meant to be the one getting the attention in the bar,' he said. 'Malvolio's the best part,' he added. 'Not as many scenes as Viola or Sir Toby, but more applause. Olivier and Gielgud played him.'

'I know,' I said. I felt like a student again. Not least because I could hear my stomach growl with hunger. 'I was awake during the performance.'

'You fainted,' he said. 'No one's been moved to a loss of consciousness before. I think this will reflect well on me. You won't mind, will you? I can change your name when I tell people.'

'Go for it,' I said. It was a poky little room. Much smaller than the one in Edinburgh, but the cool air was invigorating. On the dressing table, along with pots of make-up and a mug of brushes, was the parchment Antony had held on stage. It was not my letter. My eyes skimmed a small bunch of flowers in a jam jar, a good-luck card, a flyer stuck to the mirror, which someone had tried to pick off but on which I could still make out the words, 'Calling male actors that are looking to GET LEAN FOR SUMMER'. Antony removed his tweed jacket and hung it on a coat stand beside the rest of his costume.

He watched me, amused. 'I got your letter. It's just the fact that you're here that's funny,' he said. 'Funny. Improbable. Wonderful.' He lifted himself to sit on the sill by the open window, and rolled a cigarette.

'When did you start to smoke?'

'After I got cancer. I'm not joking,' he added. 'I'm clear now, but I've discovered I enjoy an occasional cigarette.'

I had that feeling again of an interior decimation, and I was trying to think how to ask him if he was fully recovered, how long he had left, when he said, 'I'm OK. But you don't look so good. Have some more of that Coke. They operated,' he said softly, as I sipped. 'Caught relatively quickly. I only have one ball,' he added. 'I like to get that out the way early.' He tilted his head and blew smoke through the open window. I hadn't got my bearings, but I believe we were at the back of the theatre. Despite the cold, Antony proceeded to roll his shirt sleeves, and I could not tell if the damp on his forehead was drizzle or sweat. Even offstage, his cheeks looked sallow, hollow. I do hope he is OK. He stubbed the cigarette on the window frame, chucked it into the yard or alley, and yanked the window shut. 'Let's get out of here.'

———

We walked. Antony talked. I don't remember how or what he said. Why do so few words, even treasured words, stick in the memory? I don't think it is my age that is making me forget. We had only gone a little way when I realised I'd left my brolly in the brass vessel in the foyer. 'It will be there tomorrow,' Antony said. I found it stupidly reassuring to hear him say 'tomorrow'. Mizzle beaded my hair. It would be frizzing, but I didn't care. I watched our feet, the way our steps fell together, the cracks of the pavement passing too quickly beneath them.

This is it, I thought. The thing I wanted. It is passing, the lines so fast under my shoes, I must find a way to keep it. All the anxiety leading up to my trip, the strangeness of the hotel room, vanished in this strong sense that what I wanted, I had. Antony quieted my heart. We had been walking for a few minutes when he took my hand. He did not take it in a sexual way, he just took it in a taking way. I mean, it was there, he took it to hold for a while. It was marvellous to me how right this felt. Our hands cupped, swung lightly. I had no idea where we were heading.

Antony talked and he walked and I walked beside him. His mother had gone into a home after his father died. When his work took him to Kent, to the theatres of Sevenoaks or Rochester or Maidstone, or even Margate, where we had gone to see *The Birthday Party* as teenagers, he visited her daily. He was committed to her despite, he said, her permanently jilted air. He had even put himself through panto in Maidstone just to get in a run of visits one Christmas, though that was OK, because panto was highly prestigious nowadays, and he rattled off the names of all kinds of famous actors who had done it. I told him about my dad: losing touch, the dementia that made it all too late.

'And you're still working in a library?' he said. 'What a waste.' I remember that, and I resent it. Especially as I sit here beside poor Gerald on the information desk, trying not to look at him while I type my proposed cuts into the spreadsheet. I hope I told Antony that a library is never a waste.

Then he said, 'When are you going to write that book?'

I took care not to break stride. 'What book?'

It threw me, his presumption of a hope I had never – ever, I knew that, I would not have done – confided in him, even when we were young. How would he know? We had reached the river, and as we stepped onto the Millennium Bridge, I began to think of some of the other things I had never said and which maybe he had found a way to understand. The squalling of seagulls took my breath away. Such a plaintive sound.

'Whatever book's in that sick head of yours.' He laughed. 'Ha! Look at you! So shocked. What? It isn't sick? It will be some kind of twisted love affair in which no one gets what they want but they all learn something important about themselves.' Some people get what they want, Antony, I thought. Some people stand up and sing. We all must take our stage where we find it. He tipped his head away from me and blew smoke over the river. We reached the apex. Maybe it's the feeling of suspense, the water flowing fast beneath, but I have always found bridges romantic. I pulled my coat tighter with my free hand. 'The graceful art of renunciation,' he said. I felt transported. It was the sort of thing we used to talk about, in relation to one of our favourite authors. 'Some things you can just have,' he said, 'without worrying that you didn't earn them.'

I wanted to change the subject, so I asked him about Malvolio. 'No thanks. Let's not talk about him. I have to live with the poor bastard.' We doubled-back from the bridge and passed a dingy parade: a betting shop, fifty pence shop, launderette, Quality Chippy. Antony stopped outside a pub. The Jolly Sailor, it was called. I watched his cigarette butt squib in the gutter.

He pushed open the door and disappeared between heavy blue drapes. I followed, and found myself in a small Victorian lounge. It looked like someone's front room, with a bar along one wall. A fire blazed in a corner, though it was still early autumn, and the windows were thickly misted. Antony took my hand again and led me past the counter, through a side room and into a third room. It was not much wider than a passageway. Two tiny booths had been built into the wall. He steered me to the free one. 'Have you eaten?' What a relief to be asked. He disappeared through the door to the bar.

I took out my phone. There were missed calls, and a WhatsApp text message from Kurt. I turned the phone over on the table. Light leaked from its edges and I watched the blue rim till it dimmed to an electronic dusk. After another minute, it fell dark. I picked up the phone to check it was still on silent, put it face down again, watched the light, the light fade, the light disappear. Dozens of tiny ghost Kurts glided back inside. Kurt at home or more likely at work. Kurt on Twitter and Kurt on Messenger, Kurt on Facebook and Kurt on this new WhatsApp app he'd installed for me, all asking where the hell I was.

For the past few minutes, the reading room has twitched with the beeping of digital watches; yes, many of our customers still wear those sorts of watches. Gerald, who is bravely sporting his new 'Customer Service Assistant' badge, is patiently explaining to a client that she does not actually pay his wages, and not to worry because he will not desert her at the self-service. It's five p.m., and I must hurry.

Antony returned with our drinks. From the crook of his arm, he dropped three packs of crisps on the table. He tore open the packets so they lay flat. So this was dinner! I wondered how often he ate meals like this. One of the flavours was prawn cocktail, another chicken tikka, the third cheesy puffs. I'm sure he picked them because they implied something more substantial: three courses in crisp form. He licked his fingers and glanced – I thought disapprovingly – at my phone on the table. All those phantom Kurts in there, wringing their hands in despair. Then the phone began to vibrate.

The name of my eldest flashed on the screen. 'I have to get this,' I said, reaching for the handset.

Antony laid his hand firmly on mine. 'Leave it,' he said. He said it without knowing who the name belonged to.

When the phone stilled, we lifted our hands. Our palms hovered above the phone, and then the phone vibrated. This made us both laugh, the way it seemed to have waited for us to let go before making a noise. It was a text, from my eldest. 'Dad says where are you.'

Sugar! The front door opens and shuts. 'In here!' I call to the clomping footsteps in the hall. This emptying house is making everything louder. Kurt tosses his keys on the console with an echoing clatter. I close my notebook over my hand, for privacy, and continue to scribble between the covers. How my letters slope and lean! They want to keep their heads down, and I can understand why. This whole enterprise has been underhand. I hear Kurt pause in the hall to check again that he has left none of his belongings in the closet, and I look at my notebook cover, blank, mostly shut, and all this seems already over.

All day my head has seemed to split in two. My thoughts switched to this document, this house, my phone, checking for some word, some message, some activity, some something. I left the library early, and it is now, let's see, nearly four o'clock. I could not face this next part at work, where anyone might see me. The Beaufort is empty, for now. Because surely Kurt will come home promptly, tonight of all nights.

Antony smoothed our empty crisp packets. I believe we both felt an ongoing surprise at sitting opposite each other. We smiled at one another. We did that for quite a while. Neither of us spoke. There was business enough in looking. Antony puckered and pursed his lips. He pressed his fingers to his cheeks and made firm circular movements. 'Malvolio puts a terrific strain on the facial muscles,' he said. 'In all the excitement, I forgot my cool-down.' A barman stopped at our table and switched on a little battery-powered votive for us, and Antony's murky blue eyes shone. There are forty-three muscles in a human face.

He thumbed a drum roll on the polished table. The candle began to hum. 'How long since we . . .?'

'Eighteen years,' I told him. Every relationship has an archivist. For Antony and me, I will always be that person. He cannot be relied upon to remember.

'Are you still living in Something Hill?'

'We left three years ago.'

'You divorced?' I felt he asked this with some glee.

'We needed more space.' I was not going to disclose my current situation.

'Is that different?'

'Yes, it is,' I told him. 'First you need more space. Then you divorce and afford less. You're conflating two life stages.'

'So what's he like?'

I tried not to sigh. I mean, what to say? I have visited Kurt's website several times recently, and his 'About' says he is a solutions-driven forward thinker. Last month he returned to project management to raise more funds for his creative work, and generally to live. He is tied up on one regeneration project after another. He is a sort of professional phoenix. I do hope he is. When we met, I warmed to his straightforwardness. He was direct in a way that seemed really sweet and different. But that Kurt has long gone. And if I'm honest, that me has gone too. And I do see – any time I've turned in my chair and looked at him alone on the sofa – I do see that this project makes me as unavailable to Kurt as Kurt is to me. I'd like to believe that writing makes me more present, as I feel it does, but maybe I have simply found a more efficient form of escapism.

I shrugged, and told Antony: 'Elsewhere.'

'All right. Come on then, out with it. What can I do for you?' He looked interested, and tired. A small circular scar gleamed pale on the bridge of his nose; from the acne, I expect.

I have given so much thought to Antony over the years. But I had not decided what I would say if we met. Those words too were in the dark hole in my head. I shrugged. I said something lame about getting older.

'I'm not,' he interrupted.

'You would be if you didn't lie about your age. Anyway, you look as if you are.' He laughed; what a relief. His laughter still felt like a reward. He asked if I had children. He asked lightly, as if the question were a commonplace and the answer painless. I looked him in the eye and I told him about the boys – twins, a bit of trouble with the eldest, settled now – and he told me, he told me, he had two daughters. Two.

'Daughters,' I repeated.

'Fourteen, and five,' he said.

I thought: Different mothers. And the first just a year after my boys.

'Maria – and Taylor.' He pronounced the second name as if it were still a novelty.

He reached into the inside pocket of his tweed jacket and withdrew a small brown leather wallet. He shook it open and picked through receipts, train tickets, a raffle ticket that may have been a cloakroom or dry-cleaning ticket. I have to say, there didn't appear to be a great deal of cash in there. Then he fished out a photograph and slid it towards me. 'Taylor,' he said. 'I don't have a current one of Maria.' A pretty little girl with plaits in a school V neck. I felt a pang of jealousy. Not for Taylor's mother, about whom I knew nothing, and who had prised from Antony a commitment that he had been unable to make to me. I was jealous of Antony, who had always been a few months older than me and now seemed younger. Not a young father, but the father of a young girl, which was close enough. And I thought of what would have been. I know that may sound like jealousy, but it is really closer to grief. Antony watched me while I looked at the photo of Taylor and wondered how hard Taylor's mother had found it to have that baby with him.

Here at my desk in the drawing room, I squeeze my little nub of grey speckled hag stone, and stop the hole between my thumb and finger.

A phone rang in our booth. I jumped. Antony raised and lowered a single eyebrow, one last facial exercise, and looked enquiringly around the booth. He did not reach for his phone or pat his pocket or in any way acknowledge that the phone that was ringing belonged to him. When it finally stopped, he did not acknowledge the stopping. I felt the old panic rise. God knows why. For years, all I wanted Kurt to do was to lay aside his phone and open his eyes and look at me. But I did not like sitting with Antony while he continued to smile at me as if he heard nothing. I wondered who was on the phone, and what it was that Antony didn't want to say or hear in front of me. I felt a chill draught, because a door had been pushed ajar to his large life beyond my sight, beyond that booth, and unlike the person calling him, I didn't even know Antony's number.

He swept aside the folded crisp packets and the candle, and took my hand. 'She would have been seventeen,' he said.

I don't know why he thought she was a girl, because I never knew, and he knew only what I wrote. But then I too have thought of her that way. And yes, seventeen is about right. No archivist can really number an unlived life. With our hands clasped, she seemed to live between us; we dandled the thought of her in our curled fingers, and we held her there for those few moments, and I felt, for the first time, that we shared the loss, Antony and I, and the sharing gave our loss life, which in turn, I feel this quite positively, gave a new life to me. I decided alone, you see, and all my life I have lived alone with my decision. Antony didn't speak while we sat there with our fingers clinging. No clever word. He didn't, thank God, suggest a name. You can't name a baby at seventeen. But when he took my hand, it felt to me like a small taking of responsibility. I know this because I felt some of the responsibility leave me. There we were, a little ghost family, all the things we'd never been and done, and I felt for a moment that the other life I'd never had was with me, and briefly I belonged to her, and we belonged together, Antony and I and her, and that belonging is worth more to me than any having.

You see, I always had this sense of going without as a child. Loneliness comes with that experience. If you've gone without, you know it is the opposite of going with, and a person who goes without, is without. It has taken me many years to understand that really quite simple idea, and it was a shock to me, like seeing in a mirror or photograph, say, the back of my own head – myself in the round in a way that others must find unremarkable. Antony held my hand for a long time, and right then I felt that I took my younger self in hand too. Honestly, it was more than I had hoped for. It did break a pattern for me. When I grew up, I lost a child – I made that choice. But having made it, I took the loss as proof that hardship was my due, and here was something else to hide. And I don't want to make too much of this, but in the four weeks since I saw Antony, I have not had any awareness of the ink spot in my head. I'm not saying it vanished or shrank or fizzled or exploded. There were no fireworks or anything. It didn't transform into a shooting star that streaked a golden trail across the night sky, or rise to the heavens like a beautiful bubble that burst into a thousand rainbow droplets. I haven't seen it, is all I'm saying.

'So tell me about Taylor,' I said eventually. There was a streak of tan foundation by Antony's ear, which he had missed with the make-up remover. I uncoupled my hand from his and gently pushed the photo of his daughter back to him. I licked my finger and reached to rub away the foundation. 'What's she into?' I asked. I should have liked a little girl.

'I see her quite often,' he said. 'Not when I'm on tour.' He shut his eyes while I fixed his sideburn, and I tried to process this new information objectively. The sideburns were fluffy and, now that I'd removed the make-up, a little silver.

'That's more than I see my boys,' I told him. 'And I don't have the excuse of being on tour. I say "my boys", but they are very much their own men. They are fifteen and they outgrew me long ago.' I thought of my eldest. 'What people say about mothers and sons is not true.'

'They're meant to outgrow you,' he said. 'You don't want them hanging around for ever. If they need you less, you get more time. That's the deal. That's when you write your book.'

'It doesn't feel like my time,' I said. My own mother, even before she divorced my father, never had time. After, she had even less. I was a couple of years older than the boys are now, and no technology to keep us quiet. Will I have time? I suppose some weekends there will be less and some weekends more. In any case, that wasn't what I was here for. 'I don't want advice,' I said.

'All right,' he said evenly. He had a professionally patient look that made the silence more excruciating to me than to him.

'You were my first love,' I told him.

'Was I?' He looked pleased, even though he must surely have known. He gave a slightly stupid grin. 'We were fantastically prolific pen pals.'

'Pen pals? And lovers,' I said with a snicker. I didn't mean it to come out immaturely. But I was not going to let him get away with that.

'You wrote wonderful letters,' he said quietly. 'I found them when I cleared the bungalow after my mother moved into the home.' I did not ask what he did with them.

228

'Pen pals who loved each other,' I said. 'But I'm not going to try to persuade you.' I meant, persuade you to see it that way. 'I'm not going to give myself away all over again.'

'That's funny.' He looked puzzled. 'Because that's not how I remember you. You never gave anything away. You were a mostly closed book. I was always pleading with you to come out with me, to come to Edinburgh. At school, I invited you to stay with us when your parents were splitting up. You didn't ever properly want to be with me.'

'What!' I exclaimed. 'You were the one with girlfriend after girlfriend, always sleeping with someone even when you were sleeping with me.'

'How long are you here for?' he said.

'I'm booked on the twelve thirty tomorrow.' I told him the name of my hotel.

'You only got permission for one night?'

'I didn't get permission.'

He looked at his watch. 'I should go soon,' he said. 'We've a matinee tomorrow as well as the eight p.m. I'm getting old for all this.'

It was unclear whether 'all this' meant the peripatetic life of a jobbing actor or the teenage altercation we had fallen to re-enacting.

'So you're in—' He named our Berkshire town. I nodded. 'There's talk of a few nights in Bristol in December. Maybe Hereford.'

He rattled off a few forthcoming destinations. I guess he

is a sort of travelling player. The landlady rang the bell. I held my hands out on the table, face up. 'Do you remember how you used to say we would be together?' I said. I tried to sound neither glum nor hopeful.

'Did I say that?'

'You did. When we were fifty, you said.'

'Oh no. Oh no, no, no. Oh Suze, have you come all the way up here for that?' He looked genuinely anguished. His eyes were sea blue and I tried to count the green flecks. 'I'm sure I did say that,' he said. 'It sounds like something I would say. I'm sure I behaved very badly. I expect I wanted to be romantic. I expect I wanted to make a promise that I wouldn't immediately break. Fifty must have seemed a long way off.' He sounded sorry for himself. 'Do you want to come back to my rooms?' he said. 'You've come all this way.'

I'd like to lay my cheek on the page right now. The notepad rests open. No one is home. So it's OK to do this. No key in the door. No boys in the fridge. Just us. I guess you're the voice in my head. Not my voice in my head, the other one – the one who replies to my voice in my head. The imaginary you who knows the real me. Thought pen pal, dream reader. Listening ear for my speaking mouth.

It is Kurt who wakes me. A hand rests on my shoulder tentatively. My shoulder registers the touch, knows it to be his. I hear him pick up the stone with a hole; it has rolled free of my hand. I clock the pause in which he examines it. No clues there; a stone gives away nothing. He squeezes my shoulder. Without lifting my head, I fumble to close my notebook. Kurt must see this, because he tries to slide the book from beneath my face, but the paper has stuck to my cheek. It stings when he pulls it free, like a plaster ripped from skin. There is the briefest pause, before I hear the notepad close. This he does not read.

Kurt strokes my hair and gathers it at my nape, draws it into an unfastened, hand-held ponytail, as he did when I was pregnant with the boys and my head was always over the toilet bowl. Then he frees it. There is another pause. He is deciding how to approach me. He taps my head. There's no one in. Just me in here, hiding. He slides his fingers under my cheek, and as he tries to lift, I let my head rise. My lashes are crusted saltily, as if I have been days at sea. I see my notebook on the desk, its nameless cover closed. I raise my eyes and see Kurt's eyes. Grey eyes, with those little ochre stars, as they were. He licks his finger, rubs at my cheek. When he inspects his fingertip, it is black. I have shed ink tears. He licks his finger again, rubs, licks, rubs. He is thorough. When he opens his mouth to wet his finger, a smudge of black ink gleams at the tip of his tongue. Which is funny, because I have been careful, very careful, not to put words into Kurt's mouth.

Later, we eat, and I sit beside him on the sofa, not watching while he scrolls. My left arm feels his right arm working, our elbows busy with an Inuit kiss. I pick up my phone too. I look at it so as not to look at Kurt, nor to mind the fact that he is not looking at me. The TV is off. There we are, small and dull on the blank black screen, side by side for the last time. We try to avoid talking practicalities. We try to avoid talking. We both begrudge the music coming from the Cultural Quarter. Neither wants to be the one to stand, to kick the empty pizza boxes from our feet. Two more boxes in a room full of boxes, though we have tried to be neat. I tell myself I will have occasion to order another anchovy pizza with extra olives, when Kurt visits. But maybe he will change his favourite pizza, and I will only know the old one. We stay, hanging by our threads. The sky has darkened and soon one of us – probably Kurt – will lower the blinds. One of us – probably me – will climb the stairs to bed and listen through the ceiling for the one below, listening through the ceiling for the noise of sleep. And tonight it will not be unkind to pretend to sleep.

I know I cried a lot yesterday, because in my notebook the tears have loosened the ink and washed the words from the page in long, dark streaks. When I type this up, I will do my best to be faithful. Today will be harder still than yesterday. I must keep to the facts. I must put one plain word in front of another. Hence I have come to the information desk two hours before the library opens. Here I sit alone – apart from Augustus, who I didn't have the heart to leave outside – beneath a single square of electric light. We have them on sensors. It is the saddest day. I want to be home, sharing those last moments with Kurt; and I want to be at work, avoiding those last moments. And I want to be nowhere I've ever been. I pick up my phone. As if that has the answers. I lob it into the metal bin beside the desk where waste papers break its fall. I need this time, and Kurt needs the space.

Be brisk, get to the end.

After we left the pub, Antony and I walked for about ten minutes. He told me he'd taken lodgings with a woman who rented rooms to visiting actors. She was a patron of the Palace

Theatre. Well, weren't they all. We left the shops behind, zig-zagged through residential roads. We walked and walked and somehow never found any sort of centre. I think he said we were in the Jewish quarter. Eventually we took a right down a narrow alley, and after we had passed a few doors of a Victorian terrace, he stopped to unlatch a gate. I followed him up the path, all of three steps, into the house. There was a posy of artificial flowers on a console, quite well kept, though the house was very small.

She was waiting for him in the lounge, the patron. There was a window, a sofa, TV, two full wine glasses on the mantel. He introduced her as Serena. She greeted me good-humouredly with badly dyed hair. She wore a waffle robe. Antony did not say anything about me. He just said her name and my name. I saw him take in the glasses on the mantel.

'Not tonight, Serena, thank you,' he said.

He offered me a drink, and in the galley kitchen at the back of the room, with Serena watching, he filled a glass with water and handed it to me. Water is the closest you can get to asking for nothing. I noticed a tray laid for breakfast, two mugs, a cafetière. Serena drew her legs up onto the couch, and double-knotted the belt of her robe. Antony filled a second glass. He said goodnight to Serena as he left the room, and I did the same.

The house was a two up, two down; different sort of box to mine. From the first-floor landing rose a steep wooden staircase with a shaky rope banister. The attic was Antony's rooms. I think it got the plural because a corrugated sliding door had been fitted into one corner. It was partially retracted, and I could see behind it a tiny washbasin and toilet. Where the ceiling sloped, a desk and chair had been pushed into the space beneath the skylight. There was a single bed against one wall. Antony perched on the desk. I sat at the foot of the bed. We raised our glasses and smiled and sipped.

Sometimes, in those hours between me going to bed and Kurt coming to bed, I had thought of Antony and fallen asleep with one hand on my breast, one in my lap. But Antony looked different in my dreams. Mind you, so did I. I think I had expected the years to make better sense of him. That if I found myself in this moment, I would know how to take it. He watched me, and I watched him. There were countless things I considered saying. Did you really love me? Did you know I loved you? I'm sorry if I never let you see how much. Are you OK? Who do you love now? Were you ever in *The Cherry Orchard* in South Hill? Where will you be next week? Did you get my invite to the housewarming? Why do I feel scared that someone will find me out every time I tick the box that says 'I am not a robot'? What became of Silvie? Why aren't you on Facebook? What's your mobile number? Where do you live? How often do you see your daughters? How often would you have seen ours? Why didn't you call me? Why didn't you say goodbye? Why did you take so long to reply? Did I do the right thing? What comfort did you expect me to take in a stone, geologist with a stone-cold heart?

I said, 'I haven't had time to get to the gym.' Like time was the problem. I thought, I might start going. I was thinking all this, watching Antony push up the skylight – the ceiling was low, and he reached it easily from his perch on the desk. I was thinking all this, looking around the room, everywhere but at Antony, whose eyes, I knew, would have remained avid, when he said quietly—

'I am sorry.'

He got up. Two floors below, I heard the volume rise on Serena's TV. Antony crossed the room, his head slightly bowed owing to the ceiling. I have heard it said that writing by hand slows things down. The brain cannot form the words as quickly as when a person types. But my pen is making everything go faster than it ought. The bed dipped beneath Antony; I tipped towards him. He held me and I held him and together we cried. I felt the tears rise in my chest and fall on my cheeks. One spattered onto the glossy cover of my programme. I am not certain, but I think that when we cried, Antony and I may have been saying goodbye. I'm afraid goodbyes are not a strength of mine.

We uncoupled ourselves. Antony held my hands in his, and the warm backs of his hands rested on my thighs.

'I did love you, you know.'

'I did love you too,' I said.

I said it now for then – a funny sort of affirmation, to affirm something from long ago that was no more, and in pain for something that never was. I felt like a ghost, my heart full of an afterlife love. The room was stuffy, despite the skylight. Antony's breath was metallised with cigarettes. The backs of his hands blazed through my jeans, as if he had laid hot stones in my lap.

It is amazing, the capacity of one human hand to burn a hole in another. The heat shot from my seat to my heart. Antony leaned forward. I panicked. I dropped my chin; our foreheads touched; his eyes blurred. Then my ghost self reached around the back of his neck and pulled his mouth to mine.

I did love him, and he did love me. And I thought, All this is just an old-fashioned love story, a bit out of date, but still with a little life in it. And in that spirit I slid my hand inside Antony's shirt till I snagged a nipple in the crux between my first and second fingers, that bit of skin called an interdigital fold, and with my other hand I tugged at the zip of his corduroys. We rocked and tipped and fell back onto the mattress, our heels cuffing each other's trousers past our calves. When I was down to my pants, and Antony mostly naked, I slithered towards his feet, and I kneeled. I tried not to stare at the place where the second ball had been. His trousers and boxers were bunched at his ankles. I slipped them over his socks. I peeled off the socks and dropped them on the floor. I kissed his shins, my lips following the criss-cross of red welts from Malvolio's garters. Poor Antony, the hairs all matted and flattened in those raw indentations. I kissed his knees, where the welts stopped. I kissed his one ball. The room was not dissimilar to the rooms of our youth. A bed, a desk, a window. There should have been music. When I'd finished, he put his tongue inside me and searched so hard in there. He had me between his teeth and everything was coming out, I couldn't stop it. Finally he rolled on top of me. Our stomachs made a quiet slap, although I think we were in OK shape. God knows things had happened to both of us. These were not the same bodies; yet somehow, somehow, we had the same sex.

I lay back, stroking Antony's shoulders, running my hands up and down his spine, my fingers circling and cresting the ridges of all those long-lost moles. I felt for the hair that danced. I found a few. Apart from in my head, none of the evening felt wrong, till I caught sight of those shitty scratchings. Someone had written a silly rhyme on the side of the desk, then rubbed it out so the words were leached of colour but still legible. Some stupid thing. Like, 'Serena, should be serenaded, her beauty is not faded'. (She looked a little ragged to me.) I realise this makes Antony seem childish. Also, bad at rhymes. Bad with words. Which he wasn't. At least not when he was writing to me. Of course, there is nothing to say that the person who scribbled on the furniture was Antony. Serena's patronage may have extended to other artists. All I can say is, it is the kind of thing Antony might do.

Antony withdrew and came in his hands. The gesture seemed unnecessarily evasive. Did he think, at my age, we were going to make that mistake again? I snorted as he reached under the bed for Serena's box of complimentary tissues.

'What?' He sounded offended.

'Doesn't this seem funny to you?' I said. 'I mean, I've come all this way. And this – as cheap as it gets! A box of tissues under the bed and a shitty little ditty.' I pointed to the desk.

'Don't mock my life,' he said, pulling his singlet over his

238

head. He was still naked below the waist. He didn't acknowledge the ditty. 'You'll be off tomorrow, to your comfortable house with its full fridge, where your only hardship is that you have too much time!' The force of those words took my breath away. I felt them in my stomach, as if I had been winded. He ought to see that once you've been poor, you are always a person who's been poor.

I really wanted to dress, and this may be too much information, but I needed the bathroom and I hated the idea of walking across the room naked. 'Pass me a tissue,' I told him. I was crying so hard I didn't know which end to wipe first.

He stood up. He had not yet put on his trunks, and below the singlet I could see the space where his other, his right, ball had been. He combed his fingers intricately through his fringe. It is not my place to say, but I believe Antony's fidelity to that black-and-white portrait is a curse. 'I'm sorry,' he said. 'Believe it or not, I have just about enough decency to see what a cur I've been. You looked so like you. I felt so wanted. It was nice too, wasn't it? We had a good chat in the pub. I thought the sex was pretty good, considering we haven't seen each other for so long. Technically, of course, the ball makes no difference. It's all very normal there.'

'I made this happen,' I said. I did. It must have been what I wanted. Though I hadn't wanted it to feel like this, not at all.

He plucked his watch from the floor beside the bed and wound it, surely an affectation, because I don't know anyone who winds a watch these days. 'We didn't finish discussing the performance,' he said. He sounded disappointed. 'I liked what you were saying in the pub about Malvolio as a sort of vessel for the audience's shame. It would be great to get your view on it before you go. You were always so insightful. Or maybe' – he looked at his watch – 'we could meet for coffee tomorrow. Breakfast is included here. But coffee would be nice. Guests have to leave by half past midnight, you see. Serena has a curfew.'

I nodded. I thought, Keep Serena happy. You never know when you'll need a cheap en suite in Gateshead.

We each took care of ourselves. Antony looped himself into a waffle robe and I dressed. He began to brush his teeth in the basin in the corrugated corner while I groped in the rumples of the duvet for my other sock. I desperately wanted Antony to say something. He spat out and swilled and rinsed. He flipped the mirror to the magnifying side and repeated his facial stretches. I did not look away when he saw me watching. There was something between us. Oh, it was there! In the face looking back at me from the grubby mirror, streaked with splashes and tarnished. We eyed each other, one blue eye enormous in the glass.

I do not want to live like that, with Antony. I do not want more than I had with him. But I am glad, so very glad, that I found him. He smiled. His mouth stretched, and the corners lifted minutely. It was not a vain smile. But it was subtle.

I should have thought then of my Antony, the boy I'd known at sixteen, barely older than my boys are now. I should have conjured him, found him in the man in Gateshead, dotting a supermarket own-brand moisturiser on his forehead. I wish I

240

had. But I am not sure whether our young selves were the ghosts in that room, or whether the ghosts were our grown selves. Antony glanced up at the sound of footsteps on the stairs. A firm knock clattered the wire hangers on the back of Serena's attic door, the kind dry cleaners give for free. I wonder who my boys love.

'Five minutes, Antony,' Serena said through the door.

'Noted,' he replied in a voice I knew to be actorly. He had picked up my sweater and was turning it the right way. He passed it to me, and I pulled it over my head. Together we straightened the bed. I had only a few seconds left of this life.

'You used to draw swans,' I said, perching on the neatened corner.

'I draw lots of animals,' he said with a happy grin. 'Taylor loves them. Swans I haven't done in a while. There were two on the river yesterday. Maybe we should walk that way tomorrow. Swans are fascinating creatures. Did you know they're monoga-mous? I once wrote a story about a swan in Germany who died of a broken heart. I used to like drawing the swans. More than the wolf and the cat, and the fish out of water.'

'I bet you could still draw one,' I said. I was not surprised about the wolf or the cat or the fish out of water, but I wanted that swan.

He looked around the room, walked back to the desk. Two floors below, the front door opened. 'I'm not sure there's time,' he said, as he smoothed an old envelope. 'Hmm. Let me see. Can I still do this? I have to remember if I started best with the beak or the wing.' I stood behind him while he drew. I didn't tell him that scientists in Melbourne have found that swans are faithless after all. I heard the front door shut.

'Why was it always half a heart?' I said.

He was absorbed in the drawing and I don't think he heard me. A few quick flicks and it was done. Really, there was nothing to it. 'Give me your programme,' he said, motioning to my bag. I handed it to him, and he tucked the envelope inside. I returned the programme to my bag. Antony held open the bedroom door. I took one last look around the attic. There can't be many places one visits in the absolute certainty of never returning. I felt I would remember that room for ever. But a month has passed, and already I don't. I know where the bed was, the desk, the window. I can see the corrugated door, ajar, to the toilet, the scabs on the mirror. The rest of it is just places where memories were.

The automatic lights are popping along the corridor. Mika's firm steps head to the staff room. Today she is leading our branding brainstorm on alternatives to the word 'library'. We have all had to invent one. I am quite pleased with mine. 'Trove'. Susan has told me that hers is 'think, read, surf'. I believe Mika knows that while I'm here, this place will always be a library.

I shall put this away and continue in the Beaufort tonight. I'm so close to the end now.

It is amazing how much emptier a house feels with one person fewer in it. I suppose emptied spaces are different to empty spaces: they bear the imprint of occupation, and impose their losses. Kurt is not here to not notice me, but he thought of me kindly because he has rolled the drawing room rug and removed the L-shaped sofa. Our wedding photo he has laid flat on the empty shelves in the bedroom. All my books are in boxes. The boys are back in an hour. I must do my best to finish.

Outside Serena's attic room, I held the rope banister and took the first stair. The rope bounced in my hand as, behind me, Antony began his descent. It felt dizzying to look down the stairwell to the hall, where Serena waited at the front door, her hand on the latch.

Two stairs behind me, Antony stopped. 'Let's say goodbye here, Suze,' he said softly.

I waggled my phone at him. 'One quick photo.'

He pouted to show that he disapproved of this request. However, it was the sort of pout people regard as photogenic.

I considered the possibility of a selfie. But Antony was already preparing for his shot. He drew his fingers through his fringe. He looked down to the landing and what I guess, from the plush velvet tassel that dangled from the handle, was Serena's bedroom door. He groaned. 'The light up here is terrible,' he said. But I wasn't having that. I wanted to keep everything I could from this moment. I lined up the cross hairs over his face. I tapped and tapped. I would have liked to ask him to smile with more than the corners of his mouth. But he looked at the lens, right at it, and that was good enough.

She had the door open before we reached the hall. Antony did not say, 'Give us a minute, Serena' or 'That will be all, Serena.' We had used up our time and more.

'This double header tomorrow is such a pain,' he said, wincing. 'I wish I could walk you to your hotel.'

'It's a silver Toyota,' Serena said. 'On the other side of the road.'

I suppose I should have thanked her for calling a cab, but I felt only panic that my chance to say goodbye had been upstairs, and now it was impossible to say anything meaningful. Antony leaned forward and kissed me on each cheek. He did not mention coffee the next day or that walk by the river, and, maybe true to form, I was reluctant to say anything solicitous in front of Serena, or to deter Antony, so I did what I always did. I steeled myself, I said goodbye, and I left. Out on the pavement, I closed the gate behind me. I paid a lot of attention to the bolt, so as not to look back at the house. I do not know for how long

Antony watched me before he went inside. The cabbie flashed his lights at me and I got in.

We had to turn the car around, and as we passed Serena's, I did see that the door was shut. The hotel was only ten minutes away, on the other side of the river. We drove over another spectacular bridge, and I could see the one that Antony and I had half-crossed earlier. I tipped the driver generously and he gave me Serena's address. I thought, Who knows, maybe I'll drop by tomorrow. But I knew I wouldn't.

It was so late, I had to ring the hotel bell to be let in. I showered and dressed for bed, and sat on the covers scribbling a few things in my notebook. I did that for a while before the swan came to mind. I fumbled in my bag for the programme, its cover blotched with translucent spots where the tears had landed. I turned the pages in dread. But it was there. Stuck into the spine beside the enormous black-and-white photo of Antony and his player bio. I turned it over. Two swans, sketched with sparse lines, on a skimpy biro lake. Two swans. My heart seemed to float. Each time I awoke in the night, I imagined I was paddling and sent myself back off again. I slept late.

In the breakfast room, I devoured a traditional English and pictured Serena in a loosely knotted robe, fetching his coffee in a cafetière kept warm with a twee cosy. My head turned every time a waiter or guest pushed open the door. I kept checking my phone to see if Antony had messaged me about that coffee. I knew he didn't have my number. I just kept checking. I wished I had made a plan with him. The ending had come so abruptly.

Or had it? I pictured Antony examining his skin in the mirror, dressing, me rummaging for socks, exchanging silly small talk, taking a picture. I chose the moment over the question.

I checked out at the last minute, and left my wheelie case with the receptionist. I walked along the river where we might have walked. Kittiwakes thronged beneath the bridges and the path was thick with mess, so I turned back. I refuse to say whether I saw swans; it makes no odds to me. It was dry and fairly mild, so after the river I walked to the theatre. By the time I got there, I'd racked up nine thousand steps. I was not sure what time Antony usually arrived, but I needed to fetch my umbrella. Several brollies stood in the brass vessel in the foyer. A woman was cleaning the window of the box office, and I asked after Antony, but she hadn't seen him. She did offer to go to his dressing room, but he wasn't there either. I walked to Serena's house and knocked, but there was no answer. I stooped to look through the letter box, but she had one of those draught excluders, like we used to have to keep the bills down, and there was nothing to see. I would not leave a note for them to read together. I can't write to him there and he didn't give me his number. I just have this envelope he drew the swans on. There's a small transparent window where Antony's address once appeared. But of course, all I can see through the window is the inside of the envelope. I tuck the swans back into the programme, and put the programme in my old leather case.

My heart was breaking. I returned to the hotel and checked again that there had been no calls, then I wheeled my sorry little overnight bag to the station. That sad noise. I never hear it without thinking that some poor person is lost between worlds.

I sat on the train home, flipping my phone. Out the window: hedges, cables, sky. I tried not to listen to the woman on the other side of the aisle who, I think I mentioned, was loudly video-calling a lover. I liked a bunch of things on Facebook. I watched the man opposite turn the pages of his thriller; the only person in the carriage with a book. I messaged both boys and told them I loved them and I was on my way home. I removed my shark's tooth necklace. I left an unfavourable review for a tray I had recently bought and I scanned the other reviews. It is surprising how much of people's lives you can find there. One woman, who gave the tray five stars, wrote that she bought it to use when chemotherapy left her too tired to get out of bed. 'I would never have managed without it, and no doubt I will find uses for it once all this is over. Thrilled with my purchase.' I opened an email from the website through which I'd booked my hotel in Newcastle, inviting me to book another stay. I browsed accommodation in Oldham, Hereford and Bristol.

At York, the doors opened and a couple entered the carriage. I looked out onto the empty platform and imaginary figures thronged into view. A whole crowd, a sea of heads. The dread rose. When the rain came in those golf-ball drops that burst upon the window, the figures vanished. I turned away. I was in a mawkish mood, that's for sure. To soothe myself, I opened my gallery and flicked through my photos of Antony. I'd got four. The last was the nicest. The others were dark. (I do not have a fancy phone.) His head was tilted, to show me his best side. I must say, he looks pretty good for fifty. Each image was slightly different, and as I slid between them, Antony appeared to move. I make a conscious effort not to do this too often. His lips were soft, shut. I'm not sure, if I didn't have the photos, if any of this would feel so real. More than the swan, the photos have left me something of Antony, independent of memory, and I am glad I took them. I put the phone on the little table on the train, and the screen dimmed. I pressed a fingertip to Antony's chest and he lit up, a sort of pocket Antony. I saved him to the cloud.

I checked my email, and when I saw that someone who had spammed me for years had sent a message with the subject 'Moving On', I felt sorry I'd thought her a nuisance, and sent a quick note wishing her luck. Then I kept checking to see if she'd replied. I repeatedly refreshed, to see if there was anything new to delete. But it was one of those days when you refresh and refresh and see only what you've seen. I thought of the Forum, but it was no use to me now. When I next looked out the window, the pale grey sky jolted my eyes. I wasn't used to seeing things so far away. The passenger opposite closed his book and signalled to the man pushing the tea trolley. 'Sorry, my friend, how much is the croissant?' I observed my battery decline as I leafed through my apps. I kept switching between them, thinking I was in the wrong place, that something stronger was happening elsewhere. I looked again and again at my photos of Antony. From time to time I took out my swan. I'd watched Antony draw it. I'd seen his back bent over the desk, those little unkempt silver hairs on his nape. He had drawn two swans, side by side. Their graceful necks were curved in the same direction, one a shadow of the other. There were always so many ways to read Antony. Were his two swans swimming alike and reflective? Were they two halves of a heart that never matched up? I chose to believe. But I believed in a way that was always answering a disbelief, and this made even hope feel a little hopeless. I suppose that's OK.

I wanted to swipe everything off my phone and shut my eyes.

Do you ever find you have left dozens of windows open? And when you close them, the last one – put out of mind behind a heap of other windows, behind email and forgotten searches – ambushes you, jerks you back to something you were thinking about hours, maybe even years ago? Well, I swiped away my email and messages, the maps of Hereford, the boys' new school website, and the review of the book the man opposite was reading. And the thing I saw, the last window that leapt at me, forgotten and shocking, was an article on the history of lobster thermidor.

———

It was after ten when Antony finally paid the bill. He insisted on paying it all. I recall him counting out the notes, even though, as I say, by then he had no more money than I did. We walked to the Tube, his hand hooking my waist. He stepped first onto the escalator, and as we glided down, he turned to face me from the step below and smiled and held my hand. I had to remind him to turn around when we approached the ground. The platform was crowded. The train arrived in a rush of wind that lifted the hairs on the backs of my thighs. There was only one empty seat in the car, and Antony made a show of offering it to me. I watched him from my perch, smiling while he goofed around the pole, pretending to lose his balance when the train moved. He was in high spirits. I could tell this was a special night, and though I didn't understand exactly why, and it was too crowded to talk, I wasn't troubled. I knew the car would empty at King's Cross. In the meantime, Antony looked at me lovingly. He smiled at me with thin lips, judiciously thin, as if loving me were a choice born of careful thought. They would stretch out till the edges tipped up minutely and he would show his teeth only at the last moment. It was a smile of interest. I did interest him. I believe I do.

The train gave a jolt. Antony swung comically on his pole. People began to zip up bags, scoop shopping from between their feet. One woman hesitatingly edged a large suitcase between the seats. I saw Antony turn to the window to read the name of the station, though it was obvious from the commotion that we were pulling into King's Cross. I think he made a move or went to speak. I didn't hear what. He bent towards me. Someone passed between us. The doors gaped. Then he was leaning forward and wishing me goodnight. People poured out of the train and onto the platform. I didn't have time to ask the question. What? Or why, or how long for.

Antony was swept through the doors in the crush. His arms

flew up helplessly above the heads of other passengers. He turned and shot me a look of panic, as if he were being borne away by forces beyond his control. He was carried further and further along the platform. I crossed the half-empty car to the window to get a better look. It was this moment I remembered on the train coming home from Gateshead, while the man opposite flaked croissant into the valley of his book and the fields south of York rolled past, trees and telegraph poles vanishing into my rain-soaked window while I saw in their places those nightmarish commuters thronging the platform at King's Cross, the awful panic as hundreds of bodies came between us. Did I shout to Antony? I did not. I pressed my hand on the window, that is all. The last thing I saw, before the crowd completely engulfed him, was the large rucksack on his back.

I didn't know then that he was gone. I called his hotel the next morning, but he hadn't arrived for his shift. They didn't seem too surprised. I called his mother, who thought he was in London. I left the office at five. I went to King's Cross, which in those days was quite run-down. I walked through all the tunnels of the Underground. I watched car after car unload and fill. When I finally came up for air, I hung about the concourse, turning my head each time the letters flipped and clapped on the destination boards. Those old split-flap boards sounded so hopeful. I studied the timetables. I pored over possible connections. I resented every loving farewell. I looked for him. Leeds, York, Inverness, Edinburgh. There were so many places he could be. I caught the last Tube home.

A few days passed. No word came. I raked over our final dinner for clues. Did I upset him, say the wrong thing? The days became a week, and I began to feel sick, light-headed, and I knew. I just knew. It requires a peculiarly physical kind of introspection to understand when something is busy inside you, to acknowledge that microscopic internal knitting. I am aware that even the strongest convictions of this kind can be misplaced, but it wasn't for me. I knew, even before I bought the test. Finding Antony was more than a personal wish; it was an urgent need. He would know what to do. I wept and fretted, and as the necessity of speaking to him grew, I began to worry that I had been foolish not to report him missing. Two weeks, no word. Was he safe? I called his mother again. More than vexed, she sounded irritated. 'Well, have you tried Kirsten?' she asked with a note of exasperation. I replied that I intended to call her next. Dignity has always been important to me. Sometimes I think that dignity is one of the things that dates me. This was the first I had heard of Kirsten.

As endings go, it fell so fast it outpaced even my understanding that it was an ending. In contrast, for Kurt and me the ending has caught up with us over many years, so that it is not the end I find hard to see but the beginning. As I have said, this business with Antony took place long before either of us owned a mobile. We were not the types to use a pager. If I could have called him, or texted, or just checked when he was last seen, events would have unfolded differently. I would not have decided alone what to do. Antony might have returned. We never even became parents agreeing not to be parents. He was just gone. I wrote to him, the pen a dead weight in my hand, the paper spoiled with one fat black spot where the ink kept coming but the words would not, and which to my sad eye took the shape of a seed, a tadpole, a kidney bean, growing through all those small entities that embryos are said to resemble. I sent my letter, bare explanation of our news, my predicament, to his mother's house. I waited a week or two, and then I went ahead. A week after that, I returned to work, and after another week or two, I got back to Kurt on his invite to a second date.

How long my letter took to reach Antony, I have no idea. I do know that two months passed before I received his scant reply, barely one side of paper, enclosing that hag stone. He hoped it would help me to heal. He had lost interest in geology, so the gesture felt as hollow as the pebble, a sop to our younger selves who believed in the good of stones. I guess he knew when he sent it that the moment must have passed and his was only the power to console. I binned the letter. But I was so desperate, that cool stone was a salve in my palm. In place of all the things I wished he'd given me and didn't, I kept it. A few weeks later, I set aside my misgivings and moved in with Kurt. There was a lot to be said for feeling wanted.

The boys are home!

I go out to the hall, and it is the most wonderful thing, because they hug me. They hug me beautifully, all three of us cornered together. My eldest pats my back. The youngest kisses the top of my head. 'Mum's crying,' he says. And they squeeze me tighter. I tell them I'll order pizza. Later, I'm going to show them the books on gaming I've borrowed from the library. 'I've got something for you,' my youngest says. 'Found it at the bus stop today.' And he opens his hand to show me a shiny penny.

I fear I have made Antony's vanishing feel like a big deal when actually it is commonplace these days. I have heard the boys discuss it. But we didn't know its name back then. Antony ghosted me before ghosting had been invented. He was a sort of phantom precursor. He vanished ahead of his time. But as I have said to my boys, I disagree that 'ghosting' is the same as vanishing, because the whole point of ghosts is that they don't leave when they should. Sometimes I see vividly the life that might have been. Antony remains present to me, as apparitions can.

Earlier this week, I continued to think that I might hear from Antony. I checked my various social media. I added my mobile number to my professional network sites. I usually keep my details private, but librarians are not in huge demand, and I should be surprised to be spammed. The important thing is that if anyone chooses to look for me, I am findable. I am on the electoral roll. I don't think Antony even votes. My Facebook page is in my name and my profile picture is a picture of me. I am not massively active, but I'm there. I'm easier to find than a shark's tooth.

There are disadvantages to this sort of exposure. I have lived the four weeks since returning from Tyneside in a misery of unreasonable expectation. I have waited, in effect, to be found. I have read that some people write to be found, but we shall have to see about that.

Oh, this is all I need. Here comes Susan, smiling.

Well that's terrific, isn't it. She came all the way up here to the second floor to wish me a good break. I have booked one week off. One week, Susan. Separation is no holiday. Go and run a search on theory of mind!

It causes me excruciating pain to think of Antony in the past tense. He is there in the letters, and in the photos in the cloud. He is elusive, of course. His thin mouth tells me that he admires me, thinks highly of me. He is a little weary from all the moving around. He is in Oldham next week, the picture of Taylor tucked in his wallet. After a short break, he goes to the cathedral city of Hereford. I imagine his Malvolio grows darker and more bitter; I do worry about the humiliation to which he must submit night after night. May he stay safe and well. May he always play his part. May he keep his other ball. May his heart find its fill. But I shall not hear from Antony. I have passed the points of unlikeliest and latest. I shall not see him again. A difficult encounter can take everything out of a person. However, that has not been my experience. Seeing Antony gave me something back. We are finished. The feeling is sharp and terrifying, vigorously debilitating. But all the same, I am closing the bracket.

Of course, like all gone things, the hope never completely goes. It passes, leaves behind the place where it lived, which is also a kind of life, a kind of afterlife.

In a few hours I will meet the boys – my first school pick-up in three years – and I will bring them to the new place, which is not a million miles from the old place, but more affordable to rent, being on the other side of the park, nearer the railway line.

Already something is going on in The Close behind me. While I pack the last things into the last box, out front a heavy engine turns. There goes the alarm of a reversing lorry. Sally and Andrea call to each other over the noise. And I'm sure that is Belle Glossop's husky contralto, asking how much longer. We are the first to move out of The Close, so this is quite a performance for us all. The excitement draws me to the bedroom window to peep around the blind.

The Close is filling up. Both removal trucks have arrived at once. It is another family of four, surname Bielkowski, whose furniture Akhil is directing to the turning circle. The traffic warden peels a banana as she watches their manoeuvres from her perch on Mick and Andrea's wall. Quite a crowd has gathered.

Some of the Frittellis are there, they love a show, and the Phase Three movers whose names I never learned. And here comes Mick with a camping chair in each hand. The Close is a crucible. Everyone has a ringside seat at the keyhole. Soon I shall go out there and face the audience, and I expect my neighbours will clap me to the car.

Pink and orange petals linger in the clouds above the Glossops' place; last gifts of a November sunrise. Today could be a beautiful day. I hadn't noticed till now that the crab apple tree has fruited, and clusters of rosy baubles hide in its branches. This is silly. I need to finish up. I slip the wedding photo Kurt has left me into the burgundy trunk and shut my tatty tan case as securely as the latches and wads of paper allow. Then I lift both into the last open box and secure the flaps. I have an eight-minute wait for my cab; time to make one final check for anything left behind.

I must say, the house looks good half empty. Downstairs the sisal is a little worn and dirty – at the very least, the Bielkowskis will need to book a deep clean – and there's a stain where I once spilled wine in the hall. But the kitchen units are high gloss, and whatever gave them their shine still gives them shine. Broadly speaking, I'm leaving this place in an OK state.

Kurt has left the glass butterfly his mother gave me on the kitchen island. A twist of brown parcel tape lies scrunched on the floor. I pick it up to put it in the bin, but when I turn to the bin, of course it's not there. The tape goes in my bag. I open and soft-close the cupboards. I can still see the coffee beans rolling on the floor, which is something that will not be here when the new people arrive. I will take my visions with me.

It is a reflex to go around the place closing cupboards, doors. I seal each room. I buff a smear from the closet with my sleeve. I flush the toilets and shut the lids. The house is a little less new than when we arrived, and some way short of empty, but the spare room feels much more spare than before. It is surplus even to me. In Phase One, I could view the whole grid of the estate from its window. Now the Beaufort is boxed on each side, and the cherry is all I can see, surprisingly mature in its autumn dress of orange leaves.

Outside, the engines have fallen silent. The voices hush. Any second, Ameer will arrive in a Skoda Octavia. But it is funny: I find I do not want to walk out the door just yet. I put a hand on my stomach to still the flutters. Even seasoned actors experience nerves in the wings. What a thrill it will be to step out. I tell myself I will make sure one last time that the windows are shut, a task I complete in the room of our eldest, where the musk of his body spray is oiled into the walls. I lower the blind. We are leaving those. Neither Kurt nor I can make use of them.

A few moments alone, and I'll let myself out. I will gather my shadows and take them with me. I will lock the door and drop the keys into the agent as I promised Kurt. Then I will text Kurt and tell him.

And that's pretty much it. I'll write my name on the cover of my notebook. Yes, good job, Susan.

ACKNOWLEDGEMENTS

I'd like to thank Joe Cocozza, my first reader, for telling me to keep going, and Richard Beard for helping me to see how.

I cherish the friends who read drafts and generously offered their thoughts. Thank you, Jacqueline Landey, John Patrick McHugh, Susie Renshaw, and Alice Falconer, who is always my reader even when she's not reading.

Thank you to Tony Durcan, Karen Huxtable and Alan Wylie for sharing their experiences of libraries with me, to Clive Mitchell for the stones, and Eleanor Wood for helping me to find my singing voice.

Thank you to Rogers Coleridge & White Ltd, especially to Natasha Fairweather for her belief and support, and to Matthew Marland.

Thank you to Mary-Anne Harrington, for her enthusiasm, patience, care, and understanding. Thanks to all at Tinder Press for seeing this book into the world, especially Louise Swannell and Ellie Freedman.

I will always feel grateful to the libraries that have given me a place to read over the years and helped me to feel at home.

I am especially grateful to the Society of Authors' Author Foundation Fund for the grant that enabled me to take a break from paid work in which to get my story up and running.

Thank you to Ben Clissitt, to my library buddy Elsa Clissitt, and to Gabriel Clissitt for his help with my research in Deal. Thank you to the woman in the café at the end of Deal pier who found my notebook.